# WHERE THERE'S
# SMOKE

# WHERE THERE'S
# SMOKE

## Mel McKinney

ST. MARTIN'S PRESS

NEW YORK

THOMAS DUNNE BOOKS.
An imprint of St. Martin's Press.

WHERE THERE'S SMOKE. Copyright © 1999 by Mel
McKinney. All rights reserved. Printed in the United
States of America. No part of this book may be used
or reproduced in any manner whatsoever without writ-
ten permission except in the case of brief quotations
embodied in critical articles or reviews. For information, address St. Martin's Press, 175 Fifth Avenue, New
York, N.Y. 10010.

Library of Congress Cataloging-in-Publication Data

McKinney, Mel.
    Where there's smoke / Mel McKinney.—1st ed.
        p.  cm
        "Thomas Dunne books."
    ISBN 0-312-20623-2
    1. Kennedy, John F. (John Fitzgerald). 1917–
1963—Assassination Fiction.   2.Cuba—history—
1959-Fiction. 3.Cuban Americans
Fiction.   I. Title.
PS3563.C38169W47
813'.54—dc21                                99–35875
                                               CIP

10   9   8   7   6   5   4   3   2

This is for my wife Susan, who edits my life and
made it necessary;
and for my daughter Denise, who edits my words and
made it a book.

Six hours and a century northeast of San Francisco a river plunges in rebellion before its waters are captured and tamed. Trout of mythical stature wait in its gorges. It is a place of mystery and legend. Thank you Gray Hills for wondering whatever happened to JFK's thousand Cuban cigars. Vintage as they were, I'll bet not a one of them equaled any we've shared under Bollibokka's dark moons.

—Mendocino, CA
April 6, 1999

# WHERE THERE'S
# SMOKE

*The flow of money charged the night as Raul Salazar's father hastened toward him through waves of reveling gamblers. Even at a distance, Raul could see there was something in his father's eyes, yet a new sadness clouding Victor Salazar's tormented sky.*

*His eyes locked on Raul, Victor whispered briefly to a pit boss monitoring a Texas wildcatter persistently boring dry holes at the roulette table. When he started again toward Raul, Victor's eyes lifted.*

*Raul tracked his father's glance to the mezzanine. There stood Joseph Bonafaccio, the Don, arms folded across his chest. He was flanked by his son Joseph Jr., and his bodyguard, Dominick Romelli. All three watched Victor Salazar make his way toward his son. Sweating and pale, Victor finally reached him.*

*"Raul, come and walk the* malecón *with me. We will have a smoke."*

*His father's expression confirmed this was a mandate.*

"*Domingo,*" *Raul said to a nearby pit boss.* "*I am going out with my father. I will be back soon. You are watching the señorita on table three?*" *The pit boss nodded. Soon they would have to decide whether the Texan was losing enough to justify tolerating his wife's cheating.*

*As he followed his father toward the front of the casino, Raul again looked to the mezzanine. The Don and his entourage were gone.*

*It was a few minutes past midnight, Raul's first time outside Noches Cubanas in ten hours. The freshening breeze from the bay carried a salty, but tropical, fragrance. He filled his lungs, exhaled, and did it again, cleansing himself of the casino's cloying blend of nervous sweat, stale smoke, and spent perfume. It had been too long since he and Victor had walked the* malecón.

*Victor Salazar slipped a thin, gold cutter from his vest pocket and cut the ends of two Don Salazario Presidentes. Cupping his hands from the warm breeze, he lit one for each of them.*

"*The best of Grandfather's cigars,*" *Raul said.* "*What are we celebrating?*"

*His father's eyes answered. This was no celebration. Victor Salazar took his son's arm and they began to walk.*

"*Raul, my son, my heart is heavy with what I must tell you.*"

*Raul was not surprised. The forced entry of the Bonafaccio family into Noches Cubanas three years earlier had wrought a terrible change in his father. The business he'd created in 1935 had slid like a helpless mouse down the gullet of the Mafia serpent. Only a façade of Victor*

*Salazar's prideful ownership remained, used now by the Bonafaccios to their advantage.*

*"I am listening, Father. We have seen much together. We can deal with the rest."*

*The old man shook his head and exhaled. The breeze caught the smoke and trailed it behind like a pilot's scarf. Raul thought of nightime walks with his father from long ago—before Don Bonafaccio and his Mafia snakes had clustered with Batista to infest Cuba with their corruption.*

*"No, Raul. Not this time," Victor said, his voice low and tired. "Events are now beyond us; at least for me. For you, it is arranged. You will survive."*

*Raul pulled his arm away and stopped. His father gently recaptured it in both of his.*

*"Keep walking, Raul. They are watching."*

*Then Raul saw them, shadows only, but unmistakable. The night could not conceal Don Bonafaccio's broad bulk and the squat meanness of the always present Dominick Romelli. The silhouette of a dark sedan crept along behind them.*

*Raul and his father resumed their slow pace.*

*"You see, my son, to do business with thieves, one must become a thief."*

*Raul let his father's statement linger, its meaning not entirely obscure. In the casino business, there were certain understandings, customs, and practices.*

*Victor Salazar drew slowly on the large cigar, then continued.*

*"When the criminals infected our island and our business, I knew we had lost. Those who resisted fed the*

*sharks. Better to get along as well as we could, I thought, because it would be only a matter of time before they squeezed us out completely. I took steps to protect us, our family, and all who depend on us. But I underestimated them, or at least their clever accountants. Now they know."*

*Raul's mind raced as he tried to comprehend. His father droned on in a resigned monotone.*

*"Don Bonafaccio and I have talked. An agreement has been reached. You and the Don's son are the same age. Bonafaccio may be many things but he is still a father. He could not deny my request for time to explain this to you. It is part of our agreement."*

*Raul stopped again, firmly. It no longer mattered that they had an escort. He had to see his father's eyes. He asked softly, "And the rest of the agreement?"*

*His father looked up at him, a film glistening those black coals that had seen so much. Raul read the exhaustion there and cursed himself for not attending it earlier.*

*"Tonight," said Victor. "You leave tonight. Now. They will take you to the airport and put you on the plane to Miami. You will be given one-thousand dollars. No luggage. You will be searched. You are not to return. Ever."*

*Raul waited. He knew there was more.*

*Victor Salazar again filled himself through his cigar. He expelled the smoke with a sigh. Then he turned and started to walk.*

*"Father."*

*The old man did not stop.*

*"Victor!"*

Raul caught up and took his father's arm, tears streaming down his cheeks.

"Those bastards!" he whispered.

"No, Raul. Not really." Victor Salazar was smiling now.

"For them it is business. They are thieves, but not among themselves. They have their code. I was expected to honor it. I knew that. But I was not one of them, so I did not. Now they say that unless I return their money, I must pay their price. But I know these men. Even if I return the money, they will have their vengeance."

Victor Salazar released another long curl of smoke into the lush Caribbean night as the dark sedan came alongside.

"Look, your ride is here. We must say adios. Look for some of your grandfather's cigars in the mail. I will send them to our old friend, Paulo. Go see him. He will help you get started in Miami. Enjoy the cigars, and remember me."

A door opened. Raul, now too numb to cry, threw an arm around his father. Victor Salazar squeezed his son's hand, pressing into it the thin, gold cigar cutter that had belonged to Raul's grandfather.

# ONE

"ONE THOUSAND, ALL premium Cubans, is that what you said?"

"You hear good, amigo. One thousand. Give or take a few. He has had them for two months."

"How can you guarantee they will be *his?*"

"Look, amigo, do you want them or not? They are his, just sitting up there in Massachusetts. I know others who would seize this opportunity. The way your father-in-law was talking the other night in my restaurant, he will kiss your feet for this. I owe you a favor, so I called you first. There, the debt is paid. You want them, you tell me now. I have no time for bullshit."

The freshman congressman from Florida covered the telephone mouthpiece with his hand, sucked in a huge breath, and held it. This was more than politics; this was retaliation. His father-in-law, Cornelius Gessleman, *thrived* on retaliation. Even though the Cuban's proposal smacked of an inflated fraternity prank, Gessleman had stewed over those thousand cigars since the rumors had surfaced. The Cuban was right: Gessleman would bathe his son-in-law in adoration when presented with the cigars.

Wesley Trent Cameron exhaled slowly, clearing his mind. "I'll take them," he said, forcing a quaver from his voice.

"Good. Congratulations. You will not be sorry."

Then reality seeped through. "How much did you say?"

"Amigo, maybe you do not hear so good after all. Twenty thousand." The Cuban ignored the silence. "Amigo, this will be a major operation, breaking into one of the most secure houses in the country. It will require a diversion, two teams of professionals." He paused.

"Your father-in-law would not blink, you know. He would think it a bargain."

*My God,* thought Cameron. *Twenty thousand dollars.* He would have to involve Gessleman from the outset. But the old robber baron would love that. Intrigue, vengeance, winning; these coursed through his father-in-law's veins, not blood cells. This venture would be sport compared to the ladder of broken backs mounted by Gessleman in his ruthless rise to privilege and fortune.

Wesley Cameron also recognized a distinct, practical reason to get the cigars in the family. Cornelius Gessleman was eighty-six years old, and his doctor had cropped his cigar intake to one a day. At the same time, the congressman's own obsessive craving had escalated to three or four a day as he emulated his political hero, Winston Churchill. Yes, it would be convenient to have a thousand vintage

Cuban cigars in the family. Gessleman would hardly be able to smoke a dent in the prized cache by the time he . . .

"Amigo? Are you still with me?"

"What? Oh, yeah, I'm still here. So how do we wrap this up?"

"You get the twenty thousand together. You will know when I get the cigars."

"How?" Cameron asked, leery of unnecessary contact with the Cuban.

"Trust me, amigo, you will know—it will make the papers."

The congressman thought about this. It would play nicely into the payback element. Gessleman would relish seeing the young president squirm as he answered reporters' questions about the theft of the cigars, the night of their purchase still shrouded in the hypocrisy of insider knowledge at the highest level. But publicity was always dangerous; like electricity, it needed to be channeled.

"Is that wise? I mean, the papers and all? Look, I can't afford to be linked to anything like a theft or burglary. You know that."

A chuckle. "Amigo, you are too much. You think me and some Pancho Villas are just going to break into his home and steal his cigars, guns blazing? *Amigo,* give me some credit."

There was another pause. Cameron thought he could hear the Cuban breathing. Then the voice resumed.

"Listen, I have a plan, a good one. Like a magic trick. Everyone looks to the right, and the bunny drops through the hole on the left. Get the money together. I will be in touch."

"Wait!" said Cameron. "Give me some idea *when*. It's going to take some time to line up the cash." Actually, he knew he could get the money in minutes. Cornelius kept twice that much in a cigar box in his desk, just for pocket change. But he also knew his father-in-law was a stickler for details. He would demand a schedule.

"Okay, amigo. This is September fifteenth. By the middle of November. Yes, by November fifteenth. Two months. No later."

The line went dead.

Congressman Cameron punched the intercom button, bringing his aide to the phone. "Sir?" came the pert voice.

"Get me on the next flight from D.C. to Louisville. I need to meet with our number-one constituent."

One thousand miles south, in the heart of Miami's Little Havana, sweat glistened on Raul Salazar's forehead. The horns and shouts of the never-ending parade below his office window were muffled by the blood pounding in his head. *Madre de Dios!* he thought. *What have I done?* Had the stranglehold of the embargo conspired with his desire for Rosa to drive him crazy? And that magic-trick-bunny-rabbit farce he had rattled off; what possible diversion could make such a burglary possible?

He would think of something. He had to. Rosa's fervored passion for this idiotic scheme *she* had hatched now ignited *him*.

Raul lifted the phone and dialed the international operator. He recited the number in Mexico City for Dolores, Rosa's cousin.

"Dolores? This is Raul. Listen carefully. Call Rosa and

tell her it has begun. Do you understand? 'It has begun.' She will understand. Tell her that I will see her soon, in Kingston, as we planned. I must go. I have much to do."

His eyes closed, Raul rested his finger on the phone peg, still trembling from his conversation with the congressman. Suddenly he was standing next to Head Nurse Rosa Solero at the single telephone serving the clinic in Cuba's rural highlands, his eyes feasting on her joy, his nostrils flaring at the scent of her excitement.

A week earlier in Mexico City, as Rosa reclined in his arms, and her dark hair spilled across his chest, he had meant only to entertain her with Gessleman's drunken ravings about the Kennedy cigars. Her response had stunned him.

"Why don't *you* steal the cigars for him, Raul? From what you say, he would pay handsomely for them. The money you send through Dolores is very generous, but your restaurant is failing. Use this Gessleman to help us buy the medicines Kennedy keeps from Cuba's children."

She had propped herself up on one elbow, the taut nipple of her delicious left breast brushing his chest. Her eyes sparkled as she molded the impossible scheme.

"You may not be my husband, but you can act like the husband you were going to be. Brave action is required, Raul. That monster Kennedy is killing Cuba's children. Every day his murderous 'embargo' devours one or two more."

He had studied her face, searching for any trace of humor. Anyone proposing to steal the cigars of the president of the United States had to be joking. Instead of the glint of jest, he saw the irresistible blaze of revolution.

"I will do this for you, I promise," he had said, drawn into the flame of her passion. She had rewarded him with a spontaneous burst of sensual joy that still seared his senses.

This promise, sealed in passion, could not be broken. Raul dialed his maître d' in the restaurant below.

"Paulo, are Pedro and Jorge in the bar? Good. Ask them to come up and have a smoke with me, will you? *Gracias.*"

Raul brushed aside the stack of restaurant bills he could not pay, reminded of Rosa's truth. Noches Cubanas *was* failing. Though he managed to cover the wounds, he could not staunch the hemorrhage. Labor, food, maintenance, repairs, equipment; the weight of these bricks on his shoulders had become unbearable. The embargo was the last straw. Without Cuban cigars, Noches Cubana's would lose its luster. While his customers appreciated the excellent food, they came for the cigars.

Rosa was right. Brave action *was* required. It was time to back up the bravado of his promise and the lure of the cape he had fluttered at the congressman.

Raul selected three Bolivar Coronas Gigantes from his humidor. *Magnificent plans call for a magnificent smoke,* he thought, preparing the corpulent cigars.

# TWO

CORNELIUS GESSLEMAN'S BONY fingers peaked below his chin as he considered his grinning son-in-law. Then he swiveled his high-backed judge's chair and faced the blazing panorama outside. The early Kentucky fall had ignited the pastures and rolling hills, and their leaves and grasses were alive with color. *Maybe,* he thought, *having this obsequious son of a bitch in the family is finally paying off.*

Gessleman had at first been delighted when Margaret, the middle daughter of his second marriage, announced her engagement to the young lawyer from Boston. A politically ambitious lawyer would fit well into the Gessleman structure. It hadn't hurt that the young couple had met at a Young Republicans meeting.

Then Gessleman's investigator had delivered his report. There was a pedigree, but no cash. Cameron's father had been one of the few actual window divers following the October '29 crash. He had left Wesley and his mother to fend for themselves in the jungle that was Boston's Back Bay. Fortunately, Wesley's aunt, a Philadelphia dowager and widow of a shrewd oil speculator who had prospered during and after the Depression, regarded her nephew as the son she'd never had. She had sent him to Yale, where he dutifully succeeded. His aunt was doubly proud when her young chairman of the local John Birch Society graduated from Yale Law School in 1953.

This pride in her nephew left her confident he would succeed on his own. She died, leaving Wesley ten cherished photo albums of her dogs. The balance of her fifteen-million-dollar estate went to the ASPCA.

Following Margie's marriage to the penurious young lawyer in 1957, Cornelius Gessleman had resolved to make the best of the situation. From Shady Knoll, his five-hundred-acre Kentucky horse farm, the snowy-haired octogenarian monitored every facet of the American political scene. With a network of banking and industrial interests spanning the country, he had filled one wall of his cavernous office-study with an enormous map of the United States. It displayed every congressional district, its population, and the vital statistics of each current office holder.

Three days into his son-in-law's Polynesian honeymoon, Gessleman discovered a congressional seat in South Florida that would be ripe in three years. He summoned the newlyweds back to Shady Knoll to tell them they were about to become Florida residents. They offered no opposition, nor had Gessleman expected any.

Cornelius orchestrated the campaign leading to Wesley's election in 1960. Since then, however, with his mea-

ger congressional influence tied to wastebasket commit-
tees, Wesley had been a gross disappointment. Until now.

In a voice husked by sixty years of cheroots and strong
Cuban cigars, Cornelius turned back and addressed his
son-in-law, seated across the massive desk from him.

"You say there's no way they can trace them to us,
and we're guaranteed ending up with the bastard's thousand Cubans? How can you be so positive?"

Wesley Cameron smiled. "Cornelius." Then, correct-
ing himself, "Dad." Gessleman winced.

Wesley continued. "You've seen the man's restaurant
and know the quality of his cigars. He runs a good business. Everything about that place is class—style and class.
That's what draws people like us, like *you,* as customers.
Noches Cubanas is his signature. It shows he's a professional. He has too much to lose to go off half-cocked. For
him, stealing the cigars is a payback. Just like for you.
Only *you* get the extra pleasure of smoking them."

Gessleman tilted back in his chair, the glint of antici-
pation dancing in his eyes. "Okay, I'm convinced. You
have warmed this old man's heart. You need twenty thousand dollars, right?"

Cameron nodded. Mimicking his father-in-law's posture, he leaned back, clasping his hands behind his head.
A good day's work. Gessleman's favor, finally, and a heritage of premium Cuban cigars, either for smoking or in-
vestment. In just a month, the price of pre–Castro Cubans
had tripled. In years to come, who could say? The sky was
the limit. He watched his father-in-law pull out a cigar
box and begin counting bills.

"Goddamn! This makes me feel good." Gessleman

snorted. "That embargo's made criminals out of all of us anyway. Might as well do it in style. Last week, coming home from London with cigars stuffed in my stockings, I felt like some sleazy crook."

With that, he tapped the bundle together, wrapped it in a rubber band, inserted it in an envelope, and presented it to his son-in-law with a flourish. Cameron stood, preparing to leave.

"Oh, Wesley," Gessleman said, hunched over, scribbling something on a blank sheet of paper. "Before you leave, sign this receipt, would you?"

# THREE

HIRAM THORPE WOKE with a start, wondering what that godawful smell was. Then he opened his eyes to the tented page of newspaper covering his face. Ink. *Funny. Didn't smell it earlier,* he thought. But it had not been the ink that had summoned him from the fight with the striped bass; it was the damned phone. No matter; the dream always ended the same. He had never seen the bass, just felt its surging run into the surf's foam before its inevitable disappearance.

"Constable Thorpe, here."

"Hiram, Oscar Fenton. Think you'd better shag your butt over here. Found somethin' kind of interesting a little while ago."

Hiram swung his feet off the desk and stood. Then, his wits recharged, he remembered that Fenton was the maintenance man, not part of the security team. In fact, if he wasn't mistaken, the funeral had pulled all the Kennedy security people, including the Secret Service group, away to Boston, New York City, and D.C.

"Y' don't say. What is it?"

"Well, might be somethin', might not. Hard to tell. Didn't want to disturb the Family or the big shots 'til you saw it. To me, looks like a door to the cellar of the place was jimmied. Thought you should take a look."

*Oh, great,* thought Hiram, reaching for his fur-collared constable jacket, his mackinaw of officialdom. *Just what we need up here, someone breaking into the place while the Family is away burying the man.*

"Okay, Oscar. I'll be out directly."

Hiram hung up, then raised the microphone from the radio console. "Luther?"

"Yep."

Now, *that's* a surprise, thought Hiram, already conjuring up the number for the Maple Leaf Café.

"Uh, Luther, I'm going to drive on over to the Kennedy place. Take a look around for a few minutes. How about stayin' in service 'case I need you."

"Sure thing, Chief. Somethin' up?"

"Naw, it's probably nothing. Old Oscar's got a door with some scratches on it. Raccoon, most likely. I'll be in touch. Out."

Hiram eased into the patrol car and scrunched against the corrugated seat-pad backrest as its webbed plastic memory absorbed his 230 pounds in crackling protest. He slid a five pack of Swisher Sweets from his coat pocket and wet one thoroughly, collecting the sweet saliva into a spit, which he sent through the window in a perfect arc.

He fired the candied cigar with the Zippo the army had issued him in 1943 and said out loud, "Okay, time to go to work."

"Well, Oscar, place has been broken into, all right. Doesn't take a genius to see that."

The two men stood above the storm entry that led to a remote part of the cellar. The splintered remains of one of the slanted doors hung crazily, shards of weathered wood dangling in mute protest to the injustice of such ignoble destruction after surviving two centuries of New England storms.

"Question is, who, when, and why. Anything missing?"

The maintenance man scratched his chin, eyeing Hiram's half-smoked cigar.

"Don't know. Nothin' much down there. Fact is, this part of the place ain't on the alarm system. It don't kick in 'til you get to the door at the end of that corridor." Oscar gestured with his head, indicating the rock-lined passage that disappeared under the building from the compromised opening.

"Well, let's take a look-see," Hiram said, lifting the remaining good door. He started down the rock stairway.

A bare bulb gave sparse light to the arched colonial passageway. Hiram unclipped the flashlight from his belt and played its beam along the uneven walls ahead.

Coming to an opening carved into the side, he explored the space with his light. Then he saw a cord dangling from a fixture overhead and pulled it, flooding the alcove with illumination. Before him stood two massive wooden doors made to look like the entry to a medieval dungeon. Their only link to the twentieth century was the heavy hasp and large, brass, Yale lock.

"What's in there?" he asked.

"Wine cellar," Oscar responded. "Old Joe keeps his wines there. Oh, yeah, almost forgot. Young Jack had a place built in there for cigars. Supposed to be a bunch of 'em. Ain't never been in there myself. Me and the missus never made the dinner list. Just as well. My wedding suit probably don't fit no more." Oscar chuckled, pleased with himself.

Hiram tried the lock. It was intact and showed no damage.

After poking around for half an hour, Hiram concluded he had no conclusions. Just a busted storm door and no sign of theft.

"Well, Oscar, I guess that's it. I'll write up a report and see that the security folks get a copy. Can't see that there's anything I can do. Suppose I'll hear about it if anything turns up missing. You did good to call. Do it again if there's anything else."

Hiram extracted another Swisher from his coat, mouthed it, and slid into the cruiser. Time for dinner.

"Somethin' else, Oscar?" he asked around the cigar, noting the maintenance man's intent expression.

"Got 'ny more of those?" Oscar asked.

# FOUR

"WELL, SO MUCH for Camelot," said Cornelius Gessleman. He tipped the last of the bourbon from his glass and stood. "Let's join the others," he instructed his son-in-law. Wesley Cameron tossed back the rest of his drink and followed Gessleman toward the massive living room.

Halfway down the hall Gessleman stopped in front of a brass easel bearing a large portrait draped in black bunting. Gessleman paused and studied John F. Kennedy's face.

"God, what a Thanksgiving," he muttered. "Instead of a feast, we mourn the death of a president."

Gessleman turned from the painting and faced his son-in-law. "Wesley, if some demented nut can strike down the president of the United States from a book storehouse, no one of us in public life is safe. Besides, even though he was a Democrat, he was *our* Democrat, know what I mean?"

The congressman nodded. Gessleman continued.

"Jack Kennedy's father was one of us. He had guts and he had balls. That's how he built his fortune. The Kennedys were Democrats because old Joe Kennedy was a political opportunist, nothing else. I could live with that. Things that mattered stayed the same. Now we're going to see all those eastern liberals come crawling out of their libraries again, you wait and see. Kennedy knew how to control 'em. Johnson doesn't."

Gessleman resumed his slow walk down the hall, passing the long, manor windows, also draped in black bunting. Outside, the flag in the center of the oval driveway hung miserably at half-mast, limp in the still, humid air.

"You know," Gessleman said over his shoulder, "I could even forgive him snatching all those Cuban cigars the night before he tightened that goddamned embargo. Hell, in his shoes, it's exactly what I would have done."

This was the first mention between them of the cigars since the fiasco of November 15 had come and gone. When they had not heard from the Cuban, they'd chalked the whole preposterous scheme up to an expatriate's fanatical dream. Humiliated, Cameron had returned the money to his scowling father-in-law. Two weeks later the subject had been buried with the president, an embarrassing lapse in judgment, best forgotten.

As the Gessleman family gathered in the ornate living room for somber reflection and prayer, Gessleman's subsidized Baptist preacher took his place before them. Cornelius noted with satisfaction that the two members of the press he had invited were present. He nodded to the preacher, who cleared his throat.

Somewhere in the muted distance a phone rang and

was quickly answered. A minute later Wesley Cameron felt a discreet tap on his shoulder.

"Telephone, sir."

"Who is it, Theodore?"

"I do not know, sir." The liveried houseman paused as a brief flash of distaste flared his nose. "He said he was your 'amigo.' "

The congressman shook his head. What could *he* want? Surely he would not be calling about his restaurant's labor problems at a time like this. Uneasy, Cameron stood and followed the houseman out of the room.

"Yes?"

"Amigo! How are you?"

The jubilance in the man's voice unnerved Cameron.

"What do you mean, 'How am I?' How do you think I am? The president has been shot. I'm devastated, like all good Americans. Why are you calling anyway? Whatever it is can wait."

"No, amigo. Some things do not wait. Some things cause things that cause even *other* things. No, some things do not wait. They happen because they must."

Cameron started to hang up. The man was not making sense. Maybe he was drunk. There had to be many drunk Americans that black day. Why not an expatriate Cuban?

But there was something else in the man's voice, a clarity. Whatever he was, he was not drunk. Cameron slowly raised the receiver back to his ear.

"So, amigo," the man continued, "he decreed a trade embargo that is strangling my country, that is starving my people and causing children to go without medicines and die. His grip around the throat of my country also choked off all those good cigars. He took from us those moments of each day that sustain us through all the others, the glow of a love that never disappoints or leaves us empty. But not for *him*. No, *he* sent his toad into the field to harvest for himself and his friends a treasury of the finest. One thousand of them, amigo! One thousand! This he did the night before he told the world of his crime. And now, amigo, they are yours."

Wesley Cameron cringed.

"You can't be serious. Are you telling me you went ahead and stole the man's cigars after that maniac shot him? Is this a joke, a very bad joke?"

"Oh, amigo, this is no joke. And there were no 'maniacs,' as you say. Oh no, not at all. Remember, I told you it would be like a magic trick? Well, while everyone has been watching the right hand in Dallas and in D.C., the left hand slipped away with the bunny. Only the right hand got caught. But, he knew the risks, and we took care of that. You saw it on TV, no? Mr. Ruby did his job nicely. I told you, we are professionals. Don't you worry. The operation was just a little messier than it had to be. Stupid Oswald. Had to go sit in a movie. If he had followed the plan, he would have been safely out of the country. Trust me. We are professionals.

"Now it is time to talk of payment and delivery of the cigars to you. Because there were these complications . . ."

"My God . . . ," the congressman began, then fainted dead away.

# FIVE

"AMIGO?" SILENCE. THEN some kind of rustling. Then a distant voice, a call. *"We need help in here! In the kitchen. Mr. Cameron has collapsed!"*

"Amigo, you still there?" More silence. Then footsteps, close together, someone running, more than one.

Raul Salazar willed his pounding heart to quiet. He could not afford to miss a word. *Madre de Dios!* A fitting end to the roller-coaster ride of the past three weeks. The next few moments could lower the curtain on a play that had started almost ten years earlier, a play that had trapped him on a stage he could not afford to leave until Cornelius Gessleman's greed for Cuban cigars had come along.

He tried to picture the scene on the other end of the line: the gaunt congressman slumped on the floor; the family retainers gathered around, clucking helplessly; the old man swooping in, commanding, dominating. But, who knew? Maybe not.

He tried again, softly.

"Amigo?"

"WHO THE HELL IS THIS?"

The unmistakable bellow of Cornelius Gessleman ripped across three states in milliseconds. Raul winced and jerked the receiver from his ear. Cautiously, he brought it close again.

"Ahhh, Señor Gessleman. I was just telling your son-in-law the good news. Is he still there?"

"Good news? Who *is* this? What in hell are you talking about?"

Raul drew a deep breath. This was it: *El momento de la verdad;* Hemingway's frozen instant when the matador brought all things together as he plunged the *estoque* just over the bull's horn and shoved the slim killing sword home in quest of the instant kill.

"Señor Gessleman, this is Raul Salazar. The restaurant in Miami? You remember? Noches Cubanas? Where you and the congressman like to eat and smoke my fine cigars?"

More silence. Then Gessleman, in the distance: *"Is he conscious? Look at his eyes. Did he hit his head when he fell? My God! Look at him. He's white as a sheet!"*

Then, booming through the receiver, "Salazar? Yes, yes, I remember you. What do you want? My son-in-law has passed out. We have a situation here. Is this important? Can't it wait?"

Willing himself to sound formidable, yet sympathetic, Raul replied, "Well, Señor Gessleman, some of it can wait and some of it cannot. We have the cigars. I need to discuss delivery arrangements with you. Delivery can perhaps be postponed to suit your convenience, considering the circumstances. But payment, I am afraid, cannot wait.

"There were complications. I was telling this to Señor Cameron. Expensive complications. I will leave these matters for Señor Cameron to explain to you when he is able. It is best we do not discuss it further on the telephone. You will understand after you speak with Señor Cameron. I will expect you and Congressman Cameron as my guests at Noches Cubanas tomorrow evening at six. We will have a smoke together, no? *Buenas tardes.*"

Raul hung up, exhausted, but pleased. The *estoque* had struck true. Of that, he was certain.


"Clear out of here! All of you—NOW!"

For an eighty-six-year-old, Cornelius Gessleman possessed an amazing bark, in spite of the clouds of cigar smoke that had bathed his throat. He quickly scanned the shocked expressions circling the large kitchen.

The Baptist preacher shuffled uncomfortably at the entrance; Gessleman's fifty-one-year-old-wife, Maven, cowered behind the preacher; Margaret clutched her mother's arm, staring at her downed husband, his head nodding in semiconsciousness. The houseman and several staff who had sped to the kitchen clustered in a corner near the exit through the walk-in pantry.

"Go on—you heard me!" Gessleman shouted, dismissing everyone with an angry wave of his arms. "Wesley just can't handle politics sometimes. Now get out! I'll deal with this."

Satisfied they were alone, Gessleman stood and snatched an empty pot from the center island. He shoved it into one of the sinks, turned on the cold water full stream, and filled it. He dumped the water in an unceremonious gush over his struggling son-in-law, then called out. "Theodore! Come back here and help me get him into my study."

Cornelius Gessleman was discovering something about himself he had always suspected but never admitted. He was capable of killing someone, slowly, with his bare hands. In fact, as he stared across the desk at his quaking son-in-law, he felt fifty years younger and bristled with the physical compulsion to do just that.

"You pathetic, quivering *moron*," Gessleman whispered, aware that if his vocal cords engaged, the resultant thunder of rage would reveal their awful secret to the rest of the household, now disbursed throughout the mansion.

"You excuse for a brain. You imbecile. You scrawny, pompous piece of Boston *turd*." Gessleman paused, struggling to avoid total eruption. Strange, he thought, despite the morbid circumstances, he felt a perverse enjoyment as he told the despised Yalie wimp what he had thought of him since day one.

Gessleman stopped, reflected, then went on, his tone calmed and conversational.

"So what you're telling me is that we—you and I, your stupidity, my money—are what killed the president of the United States, correct?"

Wesley Cameron's baleful look filtered through the fingers that had cradled his head ever since Gessleman and Theodore had half dragged him into his father-in-law's study. He nodded.

Gessleman continued. "And this Cuban cigar king, this Son of Castro, this Caribbean crackpot who talked you into committing my money to steal Kennedy's cigars, went ahead and killed him in Dallas just to create a diversion so they could break into the Kennedy place in Hyannisport?" A note of hysteria had edged in.

"That—that's what he told me—Dad." Cameron stammered. "Oswald, Ruby, somehow all part of it. Not supposed to come out like it did."

Then, forcing a weak smile, he added, "He said it was under control, all taken care of, that they were professionals."

Gessleman blinked, still incredulous that his son-in-law had not put together the rest.

"Oh, I'm sure of that, Wesley." Now Gessleman's voice climbed, in spite of himself. "Professional assassins and blackmailers who had the good luck to deal with a professional *idiot!*"

Again, Gessleman forced his voice to a hiss. "Do you have any idea how much it is going to cost the man who financed the assassination of the president of the United States? We'll get an inkling of that tomorrow night, probably the first of many extortion sessions."

The congressman looked up, questioning.

"Oh, that's right. You passed out before your good friend, Señor Salazar, brought up money. We are to be his 'guests' tomorrow night in that cigar barn of a restaurant. I guarantee you, *son,* then we'll hear the rest. Those 'professionals' of yours have put your skinny balls in a vice they won't stop closing. As for me, mine dried up years ago. All they can get out of me is money, vast quantities of it. But from you—a broke but supposedly up-and-coming member of Congress—you'll be in somebody's pocket, besides mine, the rest of your life. I know Cubans. Mafia gangsters, all of them. Except Castro, of course. And for him, it's probably just a matter of time."

Gessleman shook his head. "All for a bunch of lousy cigars."

# SIX

RAUL SALAZAR SETTLED into a meditative trance. Thick, blue smoke snaked aloft, spreading and probing, its rich color and aroma infiltrating time and space. Over a month earlier, when the seeds of the plan were sown, he had promised himself that his own private celebration toasting liberation of the Kennedy cigars would consist of quietly savoring one of the sumptuous Montecristo "A's" that had traveled from Cuba to Mexico with Rosa.

And now, ironically, a further celebration was taking shape, one that would have to await the outcome of his meeting with the congressman and the rich old patrón.

Losing himself in the patterns swirling from the flawless ash of the Gran Corona, Raul almost wept at the good fortune beginning to encircle him. It had not always been so.

*There is,* he thought, *a pattern of smoke binding all things. Human needs, hypocrisy, and greed gather in shift-*

*ing clouds, which surround and touch us all, engulfing
some, drifting past others in wisps of fate and luck.*

As a boy, raised in Cuba's Vuelta Abajo, Raul had
learned about tobacco and cigars in his grandfather's
fields and small factory in Havana. In early October, Raul,
his parents, and Grandfather Jennaro would push the tiny
seeds into seedbeds. A few weeks later they delicately
transplanted the sprouts to hand-cultivated fields. Then,
for almost three months, Raul and Victor tended the
plants daily as they grew. Often they worked through the
night, under Jennaro's constant and crinkled scrutiny,
weeding and picking away the pests drawn to the tender,
succulent leaves.

By mid-February, hues of light green shimmered in the
sun-drenched fields, and the Salazars began to harvest
their crop. The pale, lower leaves were carefully sorted
from those growing nearer the top, where the intense sun-
light concentrated to produce fronds robust with flavor.
After three more months of storing, grading, and sorting,
they packed the surviving leaves into bundles to ferment
and mellow. Jennaro Salazar once confided to his grandson that this, above all, set his cigars apart from the rest.
Instead of the conventional double fermentation, the
leaves of a Don Salazario were composted and aged
through three cycles. Only then were they warehoused for
three more years and finally hand rolled to be enjoyed by
a select few.

While growing premium tobacco and crafting fine cigars filled Jennaro's life, it formed only a piece of Victor's.
With each annual trek from their rural warehouse to the

Salazar Fabrica de Tabaco in Havana, Raul's father grew more attracted to the boisterous mix of that tumultuous city. When Prohibition drove thousands of thirsty Americans to take the short boat ride from Florida to visit their accommodating Cuban neighbors, Victor, then a widower, moved to Havana to oversee the Fabrica and open a nightclub.

Within two years Victor's Noches Cubanas had earned the favor of America's entertainment, political, and sports luminaries. Its success rested on one major difference between it and the Batista-run casinos: Gamblers at Noches Cubanas knew they were in an honest game. The suckers and tourists patronized the larger Batista-affiliated casinos, while the elite played in exclusive privacy at Noches Cubanas. The club had one other unique feature known only to true aficionados. There was no other place in Havana to purchase a Don Salazario cigar.

In 1935, Victor sent for his fourteen-year-old son to help manage Noches Cubanas and learn the casino business. In Havana Raul came to know *all* the brilliance of Cuba, a warped rainbow of Batista-led corruption, faintly tinged with the irrepressible honesty of a few like Victor Salazar.

In the eight years since the night the Bonafaccios had shoved him onto a Miami-bound plane, Raul had often reflected on the moment that had signaled the beginning of the end. In 1938, Batista began paving what would become a golden highway for the Mafia by inviting Meyer Lansky to run two casinos and a racetrack. The shrewd Jewish Godfather immediately recognized the need to clean up Havana's gambling industry. Its crooked reputation was driving away the trade he wished to cultivate. Victor Salazar was honored by Lansky's overture to serve as a consultant in cleaning up Havana's casinos, and Lansky's message made sense: Havana's success as a gambling mecca would benefit all the casinos, including Noches Cubanas. By the end of the war that vision was realized. For Victor Salazar and Noches Cubanas, it lasted only seven years.

On a warm, spring morning in 1952, Lansky abruptly appeared at Noches Cubanas with the man he introduced as its new owner, Don Joseph Bonafaccio.

Letting the two-inch ash tumble softly into the bronze sombrero on his desk, Raul drew slow pleasure from the hand-rolled cigar, images of the past shaping themselves in the wisps and eddies ghosting the room.

When Raul and Victor Salazar smoked their good-bye that night on Havana's *malecón,* another good-bye remained unspoken. Rosa Salero, daughter of a tobacco warehouse worker, had teased and laughed with Raul throughout their youth. Their earthy, rural life in the Vuelta Abajo had bathed them in the rich innocence of an uncomplicated childhood. By the time Raul was summoned by Victor to come and live in Havana, he and Rosa had reached an understanding: Someday, they would marry.

While Raul navigated the currents of those seeking pleasure in Havana, Rosa studied nursing and watched the quiet struggle brewing between Batista's troops and the men of the hills. When Raul returned to his hometown of San Luis in 1953 and formally proposed to Rosa, she demurred.

"My love," she had told him, "I do not need to come to Havana to be happy with you. You must return to the country to be happy with me. There are people in the hills who will change Cuba. We, you and I, must join with them."

Unwilling to leave his father to deal with Bonafaccio alone, Raul had chided her, calling her a "peasant romantic" and a "Rosa Hood." Though she had bristled at his taunts, their love was strong and she had agreed to an engagement. "You will see," she told him. "We will marry, but never in Batista's Cuba. Someday you will understand."

Raul's forced exile tore him from Rosa, who was ultimately swept up in the revolutionary storm that finally cleansed Cuba of the playboy dictator and his Mafia friends.

Connecting in Miami with his father's old friend, Paulo, Raul established his own modest version of Noches Cubanas in Miami's Little Havana. Raul had pleaded with Rosa to join him in Florida, but by then, Rosa's heart harbored a second passion: revolution.

In February 1959, following the Mafia's chaotic exodus before the ebullient revolutionaries who stormed the casinos, Raul had read of Don Bonafaccio's quiet death at his upstate New York mansion. By then, the cement of change had set, fixing Raul to his restaurant and Rosa to her revolution. Her nursing skills, once used to patch Castro's guerrillas, were siphoned into the vacuum of Kennedy's embargo. Rosa stayed in the highlands, ministering to the hundreds of children deprived of medical care and supplies by the political shroud draped over her island country.

This was all smoke of the past. Now, finally, the smoke rising from the Montecristo in his hand held the promise of the future. What had started as a simple, but outrageous, scheme to raise money for Rosa's clinic had become the key to restoring the life wrenched from him by the Bonafaccios— a way to return to Rosa and Cuba with glory.

The soft ring of the telephone intruded. The images faded and became mere whorls circling Raul's desk.

"Yes."

"Raul. We have landed in Miami. We are on our way from the airport, okay?"

"Good, Jorge. Very good. We will have dinner, a celebration, yes?"

"*Sí*, Raul. A celebration, most certainly."

Raul hung up and dialed Paulo. He instructed him to set up the private dining room for five. Then he settled back to enjoy the rest of the Montecristo, still marveling at the way layers of circumstance could bind, like the leaves of a perfect cigar.

Two months earlier, when the congressman and his father-in-law had been at Noches Cubanas, Raul had presented them both with Juan Lopez Robustos. The short, pungent cigars had so pleased the old man that he had done a rare thing: he'd asked for another, and he'd had a second snifter of cognac. Raul had graciously responded, not knowing then that he was planting seeds that were to bear such rich fruit.

The brandy and the heady smokes had opened a fissure in Gessleman, releasing poisons of anger and frustration that had been fermenting too long.

"Now, you take these, for instance," Gessleman had said, waving the dark, podgy stub that was igniting the fuse of his personal powder keg. "I *always* used to have two boxes of these in my humidor. One of the best goddamned after-dinner cigars ever to come out of Cuba. Hard to get then. Impossible now, except for someone like you, of course," he'd said, winking at Raul.

It had seemed to Raul that Gessleman and the congressman had regarded him as Castro's unofficial emissary in the United States. He had seen no reason to dispel the notion. Certainly, there had been no reason to educate them about his visit to Mexico City the previous month, when he and Rosa had refreshed their passion and she had delivered his first cigars to pierce the embargo.

"But now," Gessleman had continued, his slurred voice rising, color tinging his cheeks, "Our *president* sits up there in Washington or Cape Cod or wherever that clan hangs out, puffing fine Cuban cigars like a frigg'n steam engine while I have to smuggle 'em in!"

The congressman had looked around nervously. Placing his hand on his father-in-law's arm, he had started to whisper something when Gessleman exploded.

"It's true! I know it for a fact. I was up there for a hearing two weeks ago and had dinner with that snotty brother of his, Bobby. Cocky little squirt *gave* me one. Said, 'Jack wants you to have this.'"

Raul had followed Gessleman's story with great interest. He, too, was incensed by Kennedy's action. The president's hypocrisy had been a slap in the face in light of the moronic policy now garroting his country, his business, and his life.

The success of Noches Cubanas had rested on its resplendent selection of Cuba's finest for its patrons. With Kennedy's embargo, Raul was forced to admit that the club's days were numbered. Raul had been pondering this when Gessleman's drunken rambling had snapped him back to the conversation.

"I tell you, nothing would give me greater pleasure than tweaking that cocky bastard where it hurts him most, right in his cigars. Like to mount me up an expedition and go liberate the sonsabitches. And it wouldn't be any screwed-up thing like that Bay of Pigs fiasco. Use professionals. Do it right. Yessir."

By then Gessleman's glazed eyes and jumbled words demanded intervention. The congressman had stood and, with Raul's help, raised the old man from his chair.

"Person who could get those cigars'd be a real hero, he would. Make some money, too. Professionals, that's what it would take, professionals, prof . . ." Gessleman slumped into a stupor, and Raul helped the congressman get him to the waiting Chrysler Imperial.

After they were gone, Raul had sat at the bar, finishing his cognac and Juan Lopez. Gessleman was a rich, old fool. But rich, old fools ran much of the world, and this one had struck a nerve. He was to see Rosa in Mexico in two days. What a wonderful story to tell her!

———

When Raul returned from Mexico, Cornelius Gessleman's frustrated outburst had seeded more than a story. With Rosa's fervored challenge, it had spawned a plan.

Raul knew professionals. Hell, Miami teemed with professionals. Three days later he'd pitched the deal to the congressman. Two days after that, four dark-skinned men left Miami in a tarnished 1954 Chevrolet, headed for Cape Cod.

Again, the phone. It was Paulo.

"Your amigos are in the private room. A bar is set up."

"Very good, Paulo. *Gracias*."

Raul went to join his professionals in celebration.

# SEVEN

JOSEPH BONAFACCIO JR. let the scream of the engine level as the needle grazed 4,800 rpm's. His manicured fingers tightened on the gear shift. In a quick throw to fourth gear, things settled down, and the silver Porsche Speedster loped along at 95 mph, the tach showing 3,200.

Joseph had avoided the president's funeral by cramming two briefcases of financial reports into the Porsche and secreting himself in the Adirondack estate his father had built. There would have been too many "friends" from the old days at the funeral. Honoring the promise he had made to his dying father, Joseph now shunned such contacts, though he missed the colorful bonhomie of the "wise guys" and characters who had peppered his youth.

The barren early winter trees flew by in a gray blur, a stark and fitting backdrop for the assassination's aftermath.

Joseph rolled the unlit Romeo y Julieta Churchill to the other side of his mouth, a brooding melancholy preventing him from lighting it. One thought consumed him: *The Don, one of old Joseph Kennedy's closest friends, would have acted by now. Shit, he named me to honor their friendship. He would not have let the assassination of his friend's son go unanswered.*

Emasculated by corporate structures and balance sheets, Joseph Bonafaccio Jr. could only roar through the dreary fall day, finding little satisfaction from the finely tuned capsule of German engineering that hurled him south to Manhattan.

Eventually, he remembered the cigars and smiled. Wherever in eternity his father was, he had to be laughing at that one. "Those Kennedy kids?" the Don had once smirked. "Under all that polish, just chips off the old man's crooked block, God love 'em."

Yeah, those cigars. When had that gone down? About five months ago? Yeah, just about five months. It had been midsummer and he recalled the heat rising from Manhattan's sidewalks in waves of shimmering misery.

Dominick Romelli had knocked lightly on the door that separated his small office from Joseph's huge suite.

"Joseph?"

Joseph had welcomed the interruption. The hydra of holding companies that comprised the Bonafaccio empire spoke to him through reams of paper he had grown to hate. Soon his father's vision would be fully realized. Millions would have been sanitized into the financial muscles of the world, and the old days would be gone forever. He'd removed the Partagas Lusitania from his mouth.

"Yeah, Fingers. What's up?"

*Whoops,* Joseph had thought, *not supposed to call him that anymore; don't even* think *of him that way. We're supposed to be out of all of that.* Dominick Romelli, whose former nickname stemmed from the talented trigger finger that had eliminated many of the Don's problems, was twice Joseph's age, yet half his size. He had protected Joseph since Joseph's first minute of life and was pledged to keep his vigil until physically incapable.

Romelli had entered. "Peter Swindt's on the line. He's got an unusual request. I'd handle it but thought it would be better coming from you personally."

Joseph had nodded, smiling: Dominick Romelli, Caesar Romero look-alike and ex-trigger man, now turned diplomat-statesman to presidents, kings, and captains of finance. Joseph punched the flashing button on his telephone console and greeted the president's aide.

"Ciao, Peter. Have the Russians landed?"

"If they do, Joseph, you will be one of the first to know, I promise you." Joseph pictured the portly, sycophant, puffed with self-importance. In fairness, the man did have a busy job, so there was no reason to waste his time.

"What's on your mind, Peter?" There, right to it. *Wish people would treat me like this,* he'd thought.

There had been a pause. Surprising. When the White House wants something, they usually slam you with it. This must be a doozy.

Then, in silk, Swindt had asked, "Joseph, do you know about the 'Trading with the Enemy Act?' "

Joseph had tensed. This sounded serious. Was one of their companies dirty? If so, some sonofabitch's head was going to roll.

"Well, Peter, I can pretty well guess what it is. Sounds self-explanatory. Don't do business with the bad guys, right?"

Swindt had chuckled. "Something like that. In this case the bad guys live in Cuba. Tomorrow the president is going to announce an extension of our policy regarding Cuba. Part of that policy will involve U.S. citizens traveling to Cuba. That will be illegal."

*So far, so good,* Joseph had thought. *Doesn't sound like any of our operations are involved in anything they shouldn't be. In the old days, there would probably have been an opportunity here.*

"This means many things, Joseph. But there is one specific application that will affect the president personally, something I am sure, as a cigar lover, you will understand."

Downshifting for a curve, Joseph recalled the feeling of a curtain lifting as the president's aide had revealed his hand.

*Bingo,* he had thought. *That Peter. Lays the bullshit on for the public so thick it hides him. Then, when he wants something, he cuts through it like a hot knife through butter. Better make it easy for him, whatever he wants. At least it sounds doable.*

"How can I help, Peter?" he had asked.

There had been no pause that time.

"The president has asked me to see that his stock of Cuban cigars, particularly pre-Castro vintage cigars, is well supplied. After tomorrow the travel restrictions and trade embargo will make it impossible for him to replenish.

"Now we do not envision these restrictions will be in place very long, but one never knows. Because of the president's duties as head of state, demands are made on his stock of cigars, making it imperative that an adequate supply be secured before the restrictions take effect. Following his announcement tomorrow, we anticipate a run on all domestic sources, which will rapidly deplete them. By the day after tomorrow, it will be impossible to purchase Cuban cigars in the United States."

Joseph had nodded, thinking. This meant little to him. He had inherited a humidified warehouse full of the finest cigars in the world, reputed to include the single largest collection of vintage Cuban cigars in existence. After that unfortunate business with old Salazar, the Don had sent most of the old man's cigars to New York. And then, to hedge his bet as to which way Cuba's political winds would blow, he had prudently sent the rest of the Noches Cubanas collection north. It had been the Don's intention to preserve them to draw upon as gifts for whichever faction prevailed. As it turned out, Castro had no use for the Bonafaccios and had plenty of his own cigars.

"So, I repeat. How can I help you?" Joseph had asked, sensing where the conversation was headed.

"A donation, Joseph," Swindt had replied. "A cigar donation. The president has set some modest guidelines for me to follow. One thousand of the finest Cuban cigars. I will arrange to purchase some immediately, but do not wish to attract attention before the announcement. The acquisition of these cigars must be treated discreetly, as the public would not understand. If you would contribute some cigars to this effort, the president would be very appreciative."

"Done, Peter," Joseph had responded immediately, pleased that the administration had turned to him with this sensitive request he was uniquely equipped to satisfy. "Five hundred cigars. All vintage pre-Castro Cubans. That'll be twenty boxes. How's that sound? Need more?"

"No, no, Joseph. That's plenty. Very generous. Most of the president's stock of cigars is kept in Hyannisport. I will contact Mr. Romelli with delivery details. Is that satisfactory?"

"Sure, Peter. That's fine." Then Joseph had frowned, thinking. Something had bothered him, something from the past, something about Kennedy when he was a senator—in Cuba, at Noches Cubanas. Something to do with Kennedy and cigars and old Victor Salazar before the Don had discovered Salazar's embezzlement and before they . . .

"Peter! You won't believe this!" He had laughed, pleased with himself. "I have some cigars from a very old Cuban cigar factory, one that's no longer in business. I remember when the president visited Havana once back in the fifties; he loved these cigars. I'll see they are part of our gift. Don Salazarios, that's what they're called, Don Salazarios."

So, Joseph thought, knifing the Porsche through the lower Hudson valley, our president wound up with some fine old cigars he didn't get to enjoy. I wonder if he smoked any of the Don Salazarios? Probably not. He would have called me. Hope Teddy or Bobby enjoy them. Wouldn't hurt if they knew where they came from. Sure remember the big deal about them when the senator was in Cuba. Haven't smoked one since then. Maybe I should in honor of the poor bastard. I think there's still a box of 'em in the humidor room at the office.

The thought cheered him and he pulled over to light the Churchill. As he did, he thought again of Victor Salazar. The miserable wretch had died horribly, taking his three-million-dollar secret with him.

# EIGHT

CENTRAL PARK SPARKLED below, the full moon refracting particles of November frost into infinitesimal points of light. Joseph Bonafaccio collapsed onto the massive leather couch, worn by the monotonous drive but anticipating the Manhattan night ahead. First Sardi's, then the Stork Club, then, well, the evening would take its own shape. It always did.

But first, a shower and a cigar, a Don Salazario.

Still wrapped in a thick terry cloth robe, Joseph toweled his hair and crossed to the couch, humming. Dominick Romelli stepped from the walk-in humidor and closed the glass door etched with a lazy, gracefully curved palm tree.

"I found them, Joseph. You were right. There was one box left here. Presidentes. The other three boxes from the warehouse went to Hyannisport for the president."

Joseph beamed. Discovering a lost vintage cigar was like a personal rebirth.

Carefully, he pried open the box. Then he lifted the lid and absorbed the rich fragrance that had waited inside for at least ten years.

"Ahhhhh! Dominick, take in some of that," he said, offering up the opened box. "Better than—well, lots of things." Joseph still struggled with vulgarity in front of the man who had virtually raised him.

He pulled the ribbon that released the first cigar. Then he teased out another, for Romelli.

Joseph lapsed into silence, letting the luscious smoke spread around them. Havana seemed so close again. Those slow, wonderful days; the long, tropical nights . . .

Romelli followed his lead and the two smoked in silence, the twinkling lights below as jewels masking the city's darker secrets. Finally, Romelli spoke.

"Joseph, you've had something on your mind, right? I've noticed, this past month, something's eating at you. What's up?"

A long hush of smoke escaped Joseph's mouth. He rose and walked to the picture window framing Central Park. He leaned his forehead against the glass, his hands clasped behind him. The Don Salazario rested between the thumb and cupped fingers of his right hand.

"Dominick, you don't miss much," he said, looking out over the park. Then he turned and faced the man his father had trusted to shield him from the past.

"It started before Kennedy was killed, but since then it's become ten times worse. It's—it's this *business,* you know? Here I've got these goddamn degrees from Columbia, I run an empire of movie companies, trucking lines, theaters, two casinos, and an insurance company—I'm chairman of the board of four companies and on the boards of ten or twelve others, not to mention the goddamn charities—shit, I can't even remember them all. And you know what?"

Romelli started to nod, his eyes closed.

"Right. You *do* know, don't you?" Joseph asked. "I'm going crazy! I feel so goddamn *useless!*"

Romelli laid his cigar in the onyx ashtray on the thick, glass table in front of the couch and spread his hands across his knees. "Joseph . . . ," he began.

"Wait. You asked. Let me finish," Joseph said.

"All I do is manipulate numbers with loaded dice. This—this conglomerate my father started—hell, he would've ended up a screaming lunatic in a padded cell if he'd had to run it. In his day, business was cash, business was people, and, yeah, sometimes business was blood.

"I'll tell you, Dom, I would've been a hell of a lot better at doing things my father's way than I am in this world of bean counters and 'Yes' men."

Joseph stopped and drew on his cigar. He continued in a flourish of smoke.

"Tell you something else, Dom. The Don would have known by now who was responsible for that mess in Dallas and would be doing something about it. He wouldn't be sitting back watching Warren and these old ladies with their goddamn commissions and investigations pussyfooting all over the place while the assassinating sonsabitches who shot our president are getting away with it. Hell, we know that commie Oswald was just a stupid triggerman."

Their eyes met.

"Sorry," Joseph mumbled. "No offense. What I meant was a real pro like yourself would never have been caught. Somewhere out there the assholes who orchestrated the thing are laughing at all of us. Oswald was a joke. No way he did this alone."

Another long draw on his cigar. Then, a caged cat, Joseph began pacing the span of the window, smoke trailing, words spewing.

"Not only was my father close to Kennedy's father, he knew about government and business, *his* business. You've *got* to have stable government to do good business. Anarchy is *bad* for business. Can't have assholes running around shooting the president. Just can't have it! Shit, you've seen what's happened to the stock market since the assassination. We've lost millions! I know things'll straighten out, but the peaks and valleys that follow this kind of thing are terrible. We're not in control when some kook with a rusty rifle can blow everything to shit in a few seconds."

Joseph shook himself and sat down. "So, you wanted to know what's been bugging me? Now you know. I feel like a goddamned *eunuch!*"

The ash on Joseph's cigar had reached a full two inches. He reached across the gleaming receptacle and let the spent leaf fall. But it didn't just fall, it clinked.

Joseph stared. Ashes do not clink.

There, in the crumble, shimmering against the ebony of the ashtray, rested a large diamond.

For Joseph Bonafaccio, with the millions he controlled, the sparkling gem was, at first, simply a puzzle.

Pondering it, shards of memory triggered by Kennedy, Havana, and the Don Salazarios crackled electrically into life. Suddenly they spelled a name: Victor Salazar.

Under the startled gaze of Dominick Romelli, Joseph shredded the remains of his cigar. The rubble of tobacco produced nothing more. Then he snatched Romelli's and began to tear it apart. Another glistening jewel rolled from the tattered leaves.

In silence, Joseph and Romelli destroyed the remaining Don Salazarios. Each yielded a clear, sparkling diamond. When they finished, a mound of twenty-five gems shot lasers of red, blue, and gold off the surface of the onyx bowl.

While Joseph had little doubt the diamonds were genuine, he had to be sure. Herman Meyer, jeweler to the Bonafaccios for decades, and their fence when necessary, was a phone call and twenty-minute cab ride away. Joseph picked up the phone.

Within the hour, the short, bald jeweler sat before them. Beads of sweat oozed from the wrinkles of pink skin mounded above his sparse eyebrows. At last he looked up, relaxed the ocular pressure clamping the jeweler's loupe in place, and let the silver tool tumble to his chest.

"Oh, my. My, my, my, Joseph, I will not even try to find a reason to discount these. They are perfect. All of them. I will be honored to purchase them from you. And, the rest, as you say, when you acquire them. My price to you, tonight, $30,000 each. $750,000 for these twenty-five stones. I have clients and associates who will be pleased to purchase them from me. If the rest are of the same quality, you may count on that price for them. How many did you say? Seventy-five?"

The lumpy jeweler squeezed his eyes shut for several seconds, then opened them, smiling. "That would be $2,250,000."

Joseph sat back, his fingers peaked beneath his chin.

Meyer continued. "Such cutting! I tell you, a master did this work. A true master. There have been only a few with this talent in the past several decades. I suspect, but cannot be sure without actual comparison, that these stones were cut by Javier Menendez, a Spaniard who worked for Winston's here in New York. These stones are what is called 'Ideal Cut.' Winston's perfected it.

"This fellow, Menendez, absconded with a fortune in uncut diamonds about fifteen years ago. There were rumors he turned up in the Caribbean and possibly Cuba. But they were only rumors. These twenty-five stones and the seventy-five more of them you mentioned would approximate what he got away with. Then the retail value, when cut, was around $2.5 million."

*Yes,* thought Joseph Bonafaccio, *that crafty old Victor Salazar embezzled three million dollars from my family, converted it into diamonds, and had that tobacco farmer father of his roll them up in cigars to get them out of Cuba. Only he'd run out of time. Salazar had fed the sharks, and the cigars slept for all these years in the vast Bonafaccio collection. That is, until three weeks earlier when Joseph sent Dominick to Hyannisport to personally deliver three boxes of them to the president. Jesus!*

Joseph felt the flare of a raging heat, the blood of generations of men who were never bested. The urge for vengeance and restitution seized him. Finally! A chance to show some balls!

Though Victor Salazar had paid horribly for his treachery, the fruit of his crime had now surfaced. What had been stolen from the Bonafaccio family would be retrieved. But there was the problem of face: approaching the Kennedys and asking that the three boxes of Don Salazarios be returned was unthinkable.

"Fingers! Goddamn it! Get some soldiers together. You're going to Hyannisport! Now!"

# NINE

RAUL CLOSED THE doors to the private banquet room and turned to greet his guests, Juan, José, Pedro, and Jorgé. The four sat sprawled with the arrogance of conquerors. The box of Romeo Y Julieta Fabulosos Raul had instructed Paulo to leave on the table was open, and a dizzying ether of rum and smoke filled the room.

"Heros! Welcome!" Raul cheered, circulating and hugging each of them. He lit one of the cigars for himself and poured out a generous helping of rum. Then he settled into one of the overstuffed chairs, leaned forward, and, in the conspiratorial tone of a pirate, said, "All right, lads. Out with it. The whole story."

Four sets of gleaming teeth flashed back at him. Finally, Jorgé spoke. "Ah, Raul, Raul. From such a troubled start to such a glorious finale. Your call to us that day, the day of the assassination, masterful! We were packed, ready to leave the motel, on our way to the airport, our heads hanging in shame and failure. Two weeks we had waited, working, searching for a way. I mowed lawns. Juan washed dishes and helped with the mowing. José cleaned fish at a market. Pedro, well, Pedro, he . . . what *did* you do, Pedro?"

Robust laughter erupted from the three. Pedro shook his lowered head.

"Oh, yes. I remember! Pedro met a señorita! What was her name? Ah! Felicia! She works for the Kennedys, a maid. So he was trying to do his part. And, as it happens, he did, or she did. You will hear."

Clearing his throat with rum, Jorge continued.

"The place was impossible! People everywhere. *Policia,* guards. The skinny brother's wife was there with her kids. Dozens of them! These people breed like Puerto Ricans! Then, just as we were prepared to give up, to crawl back to you in disgrace, Dallas happened, and you called. I will never forget your words. 'When they leave for the funeral, you go.' Just like in a commando movie.

"We went in three nights later, after the place emptied out. We knew exactly where to go. Pedro's señorita, the maid Felicia . . . Oh, but I will let the lover, Pedro, tell you that part."

"No trouble? None at all?" Raul asked.

"None!" Jorge proclaimed. Then he darkened. "Well, there was the door, but . . ."

"Door?" asked Raul, preparing for the worst.

"As we were leaving, an old door for storms, a door to the basement where the cigar room was. It came down on poor Juan's head. So he . . ."

"I smashed it," Juan muttered sheepishly. "With a rock. Then I threw the rock into the sea. No prints."

"Is that all? A smashed door?" asked Raul.

"Well, there was my head," Juan said ruefully.

"And the cigars?" asked Raul. "I presume they are safe?"

"*Sí*, Raul," replied Jorge. "As you told us, we stored them up there. The motel had no business and the goofy *cabrón* that owned it was happy to rent us a room for another two weeks. The cigars will be safe there. It would have been too risky to carry them with us or send them down here. We can deliver them to Señor Gessleman up there. Let *him* live with that risk. You were right."

Jorge smiled and looked at his three comrades, who all nodded, encouraging him. Raul could see there was more.

"What else?" he asked.

Jorge winked. "On the count of three," he said to the others, his wide grin growing impossibly wider. *"Uno, dos, tres!"*

With that, he reached behind his chair and produced a box of cigars. Pedro and Juan did the same. The three men extended the boxes to Raul, who gasped, recognizing at once his grandfather's distinctive *marque*.

*"Madre de Dios!* Don Salazarios! And Presidentes at that! Where have these come from?"

Pedro proudly answered, "Ironic, eh? They were part of the president's cigars. We knew you would want them, so we brought them with us. They should be yours, not this Señor Gessleman's."

Raul ran his hand over the three exquisite boxes set before him. The mitered joints, delicate brass hinges, and hand-embossed design surrounding his grandfather's *marque,* an elegantly attired gaucho waving his hat from an immense, rearing stallion, heralded the quality of the cigars inside. Jorge was correct, and he had meant well. They should be Raul's as a right of heritage. But they were not. Unless . . .

"Ah, my friends," he said, misting, "you have done so well. And to honor me with such a gift. I cannot find words."

In truth, Raul could not find the words to tell them that he would not be able to keep the Don Salazarios, not like this.

Raul Salazar's early years on his grandfather's tobacco farm, tempered by the rich theater of human nature played out in his father's casino, had left him with a conscience labrinthed with chambers of rationalization and a unique, philosophical sense of justice. Casting a scenario that left Cornelius Gessleman and the congressman believing they had subsidized the president's assassination had been a simple marriage of fate, timing, and opportunity. Between Gessleman's lust for the Kennedy cigars and, now, Gessleman's fear of exposure for the role he believed he had played in the president's death, Raul would generate the cash he needed to be rid of his declining restaurant and join Rosa, forever.

But substituting three boxes of some other cigars for the Don Salazarios was, to Raul, an inexcusable fraud. No compartment of Raul Salazar's complicated conscience housed *that* degree of duplicity. A bargain was a bargain. He would deliver to Gessleman and the congressman the *actual* cigars gathered through Kennedy's guile. The president's death and the knowledge already seeping through interested circles about Kennedy's embargo-eve mendacity made the cigars uniquely valuable to Gessleman. Raul would not cheat him of that perverse pleasure.

Perhaps, thought Raul, *another* bargain could be made. One by which he could honestly claim one of the boxes bearing his grandfather's *marque*. What a thing that would be, if someday he had a son and was able to present him with a box of cigars rolled by his great-grandfather!

Raul blinked himself back to the moment.

"How can we be sure that the cigars you took are the thousand cigars Kennedy obtained before the announcement?" he asked. "Our 'clients' may want to know that."

Jorge nodded toward Pedro, giving him center stage.

Pedro answered, grinning. "Number one, there were no other cigars in the room. Just those: 992 cigars. A few of the boxes had been opened."

Pedro paused, gesturing toward the three boxes in front of Raul. "Fortunately for you, the Don Salazarios were still sealed.

"Number two, Felicia, sweet Felicia. She loved it that I smoked cigars. She told me that she had helped the president's aide and a man who looked like a movie star carry a lot of cigars to a room in the basement from the back of the aide's car and a big Cadillac the man was driving. That's how we knew exactly where to strike. After she saw my love for cigars, she sneaked me into the basement one night to show me all those fine cigars!"

"Amazing!" declared Raul, laughing. "Such talent! And the Señorita Felicia? What of her now? Just a fond memory or is there something else?"

Pedro averted his eyes, smiling.

"Pedro, Pedro. Be very careful, my friend. We all . . . Ah, I do not have to tell you. You will use excellent judgment, I know. Well, my friends, you deserve a feast." Opening the doors, he called, "Paulo, we are hungry!"

# TEN

"CONSTABLE THORPE HERE." Hiram lifted his wife's leg from his thigh, which brought her snoring to a snagged halt. He propped himself up on an elbow and looked at the clock. The luminous hands pointed to 4:07. His wife rallied and the snoring revived.

"Hiram? Oscar Fenton again. Sorry to bother you so early, but well, you did say to call if there was anything else. And there is. Oh, yesiree, there is. Think you should get out here soon as possible."

"Want to tell me a little now?" Hiram asked. He cradled the phone as he shrugged on his shirt and reached for his pants, alerted by the excited pitch of Oscar's voice.

"Well, you remember the storm doors? One was all busted up? And the big doors to the wine room? The ones with the big lock?"

"Yes, yes, Oscar. I remember. What about them?"

"Hiram, it's the damnedest thing. Those storm doors

are gone. Plumb gone. And the wine room? It's a mess! Everything's all ass-over-teakettle. The lock's been hack-sawed and . . . oh, hell, you just better get on out here."

Hiram shut off the rotating beacon as he pulled into the Kennedy compound. Again Luther had surprised him. He was already there. *That's twice in two days now,* Hiram thought. *Better watch out for my job.* He parked along-side Luther's patrol car and stepped into the wet, morning darkness.

"Howdy, Hiram!" chirped his deputy, clearly ener-gized by the magnitude of the event.

"Settle down, Luther," Hiram muttered. "Don't want to get everyone too excited, do we?" He angled his head toward the half-dozen staff, some in bathrobes, huddled in the early dawn.

"Let's see what we've got here," he said, setting off for the storm opening.

A half an hour later he knew no more than when he'd hung up with Oscar. Standing in the middle of one of the expansive lawns, trying to decide what to do next, Hiram felt a gentle pull at his sleeve. He turned and found himself looking into eyes darker, softer, and prettier than any he had ever imagined.

"Yes, Miss?" he asked.

"Señor Constable, excuse me. I do not wish to bother you, but . . ."

Enchanted, Hiram studied the slender, young woman. Her copper skin and black eyes captivated him completely. "Oh, that's quite all right, Miss. Is there something you want to say? Why don't we start with your name."

"I am Felicia Mercado, one of the downstairs maids. I . . . I . . ." Her eyes lowered.

Hiram turned and faced the water. Even the golden glow of her exquisite skin could not cover the blush reddening her cheeks. Out of the corner of an eye he saw that she also had turned toward the sea. She started again.

"About two weeks ago a man came to visit another man who had been hired to help the gardeners. The man's name was Pedro. The helper was Jorge.

Hiram resolved to let her have her say without prompting. As she started to talk, she seemed to gain some momentum. Besides, he could not interrupt a voice that had the loving, sweet richness of a viola.

"I brought iced tea to the gardeners and met Pedro. He was a very nice man, very handsome. We talked and laughed. He was very funny and teased me. I liked him."

Hiram began to sense where this was going. He let her continue.

"We went to dinner and the movies. Several times. We became . . . close. He talked of finding work and moving here from Mexico, where he said he was from. But I think he was not. I am Mexican. I think he was from Cuba. There is a great difference in the accent."

Suddenly the words were tumbling and Hiram looked down at her. Tears filled her eyes, but still the words came.

"He loved cigars and smoked them all the time. I wanted to please him so one night, when none of the family was here, I took him into the basement and showed him all those beautiful cigars, the ones I helped the gentlemen take into that room some months ago. It made him very happy. But then I saw him only one more time."

After a pause, Hiram cleared his throat and started to fill in some blanks. He obtained descriptions of Pedro, Jorge, and one other who had helped the gardeners. She did not know his name. Then he asked her to tell him about the men she had helped with the cigars.

"Oh," she said, brightening. "One of them, Señor Swindt, is here all the time. I am sure you know who he is. The other, a short, heavy man with wavy, gray hair, like a movie star, but he looked also like a *luchador* . . . how do you say . . . ?" She made grappling gestures.

"Wrestler?" Hiram asked.

"*Sí!* Like a wrestler," she answered.

"I had never seen him before. He arrived here one afternoon about the same time as Señor Swindt. He was driving a very beautiful big, black car. A Cadillac, I think. There were many boxes of cigars in both cars, and I helped the two of them take them into the room in the basement where the wine and cigars are kept."

As they walked toward the patrol cars, Luther could not contain himself. "Jeeez! What a morning. First, those three guys, and now this!"

Hiram stopped. "What three guys, Luther?"

"The three guys roaring down the highway lickety-split in the biggest black Cad I've ever seen! That's who. Passed by me as I was coming out here to meet you. If I hadn't been so gosh durned in a hurry to get here, I would've run 'em down and given 'em the ticket they de-served!"

Hiram dug into his mackinaw for a cigar. Empty. It was going to be one of those days.

# ELEVEN

"BOSS . . . JOSEPH, I tell you. There wasn't a cigar in the place. Just wine. Lots of it. And we really took the place apart. If there had been so much as a cigarette, we would have found it. I helped Peter and one of the maids put the whole lot in there when I delivered yours. We stacked them on shelves, at least thirty or forty boxes of cigars, including the three boxes of Don Salazarios. We made a big production of putting the Salazarios right up front where he would see 'em."

Joseph Bonafaccio Jr. regarded his trusted Dominick pensively, trying to sort out what this meant. Where else could they be? There was no way the president could have smoked them or given them away in four months.

Romelli walked over to the huge picture window and ran his fingers through the wavy, peppered mass that had spawned a second nickname, "Caesar."

"It was an odd setup, Joseph," he said, studying the early skaters below. "It was like no one cared. There was this storm door, all freshly busted up. I mean, the Kennedys, right? They're not just going to leave a ramshackle door hanging on its hinges. The place is out of a picture book, everything spit and polish. Except the stupid storm door. Which, by the way, isn't there anymore. We took it with us. Both of them. They became firewood."

Joseph raised his eyebrows, questioning.

"It was kind of a goof-up. Angelo, he tripped on one of the broken boards and crashed over into the doors. He hadn't put his gloves on yet, and he left prints all over the place. Rather than try to wipe them down, I figured it was safer to just take them. So we did.

"But that's not all that was weird. When we got to the place where the wine and cigars are kept, Angelo couldn't pick the lock."

Romelli slammed a stubby fist into his other palm.

"Joseph, someone who knew his business had *already* picked that lock; I'd swear it! It's a screwy kind of lock. I've seen them before. Lots of times when they've been picked and then relocked, they jam. You can't unlock them, and you sure as hell can't pick them. Angelo tried every trick in the book, and he knows them all. We sawed it. Had no choice."

Joseph Bonafaccio Jr. let this sink in as his mind expanded into the dark mystery of the night beyond. Then, in his father's low voice, he said, "Sit down, Fingers, let's add this up. See where we are."

Dominick Romelli left the window and took a seat in front of Joseph's ornate Louis XIV desk. Chastened, he waited.

"Here's the way I see it," Joseph began.

"Number one, there are millions stuffed in cigars out there somewhere. *Our family's* cigars. *Our family's* millions, stolen from us in Cuba by that snake, Victor Salazar.

"Number two, they know there's been a break-in. The Kennedys, the cops, probably by now the goddamned CIA. Do they know why? No. How could they? Unless . . . shit. What if *he,* the president, lit up one of those diamond-loaded suckers? Or he gave one to some Arab or some other puffed-up potentate? Jesus!"

Joseph caught his breath, then continued, putting those possibilities aside for the moment. If the diamonds had been discovered by Kennedy, the problem had no solution, at least none immediately apparent.

"Number three—and this is the ball buster—someone beat us to them. Someone else knows and has our goddamned diamonds!"

His fist slammed down on the inlaid surface of the desk. A row of silver frames, housing photographs of the Don and Joseph Junior mugging with world leaders and celebrities, cascaded into each other, silver dominoes elegantly toppling. The last, a picture of a young Senator Kennedy and a bony Frank Sinatra, flanked by Joseph and his father, Noches Cubanas and the Havana skyline sparkling behind them, fell with a gentle plop to the thick carpet below. Romelli bent down and picked it up.

"Joseph, this isn't like you," he said, starting to right the fallen photographs.

Joseph nodded. "You're right, Dominick. The Don

never got mad. He just got even. No matter how long it took. Only one man ever put one over on him and that was Salazar. He paid a hell of a price, didn't he?"

He tilted back, hands behind his head.

"The Don was right to send me out in the boat with you that morning. I learned more then than in seven years at Columbia. Business, *our* business, was tough sometimes. People didn't get away with cheating us. They stole from us, they lost, no matter who they were. Like Salazar. Hell, the Don loved the guy! We all did. It didn't matter. He cheated us; he had to pay.

"I remember the look on your face when you shoved the poor bastard over. That was awful, with the guy still squirming and kicking. Jesus, life left him hard!

"And when those first sharks hit, the look on *his* face. Beat up as he was, I'll never forget that look."

Joseph stood, shaking off the memory of that long-ago morning on Havana Bay. He walked over to the humidor room, slid open the thick, glass door, and stepped into the redolence of Spanish cedar paneling and aged tobacco.

Standing with his hands folded in the small of his back, slowly moving along the rows and stacks of boxes, an antiquarian in search of a rare volume, he called over his shoulder to Romelli. "Dominick, what we do now is simple. We do what the Don would have done. Pick up the pieces. Put the puzzle together. Get what's ours."

Joseph browsed the shelves of boxes, touching, opening. Finally he settled on a box and nodded in satisfaction.

"Victor Salazar's son, what was his name? Raul, wasn't it? Didn't he open up a place in Miami some time after we kicked him out of Cuba? Same name as the old place. Seems to me I heard he had an excellent selection of Cuban cigars down there. We should pay him a visit and see if he knows anything about cigars with diamonds in 'em."

Joseph stepped back and paused at a guillotine device mounted on an alabaster pedestal. He inserted the end of one of the cigars he had selected into the opening and gave a short flick of the handle alongside. He passed the cut cigar to Romelli.

"Here, a Saint Luis Rey Regios Robusto. Perfect before lunch."

He repeated the operation on the other cigar, lit it, and started to slip on his topcoat.

"If it weren't for my date tomorrow night with that Rockette, I'd say we should fly to Miami in the morning."

# TWELVE

Raul watched from above as the congressman stepped from the cavernous rear of the Imperial into the muggy Miami evening. The owl-faced old man with him hovered at the edge of the seat, eyes darting, scanning the windows and rooftops of the buildings along the Avenida de Heros.

*Wonderful,* thought Raul. *Last night I celebrated with comrades, proud and full of themselves. Tonight I meet with quivering pigeons. Look at the old man. He is terrified. I wonder—because he believes we shot Kennedy, does he think we are going to shoot him, too? Look at him! Using his son-in-law as a shield. Disgusting! But it is best he is frightened and unsure of himself. It helps our cause.*

Then, as the congressman and Gessleman disappeared below into the entrance to Noches Cubanas, Raul thought again of the three boxes of Don Salazarios. Spreading his most congenial smile, he went down to greet his guests.

"Señores, welcome," Raul said, extending his hand toward the congressman. Paulo opened the doors for them to the private dining room. Raul's guests paused; then Gessleman nudged his son-in-law ahead, toward the room.

A faint, "Mr. Salazar," escaped Wesley Cameron, who started to accept Raul's handshake. He abruptly retracted his arm as his father-in-law's look cleared the space it would have occupied.

Raul folded his arms but maintained his smile. All who entered Noches Cubanas were treated with respect and congeniality. These guests, here to be blackmailed, would be treated like royalty.

"Please, gentlemen. Be seated." His arm swept toward the table set in the middle of the room. Cut-crystal wine glasses and water goblets reflected the rich hues of china plates bordered with gilt tobacco leaves. At each of the three place settings, a fan of five cigars spread tan-and-dark fingers from a round sterling match safe that housed a dozen thick, wooden matches.

"I have instructed our kitchen to prepare several of our finest dishes for you. As you see, a selection of beautiful cigars awaits your pleasure."

Gessleman squinted to get a better look at the cigars. "All very impressive, Mr. Salazar. Very impressive. But under the circumstances, we are *not* staying for dinner. Now let's cut the generous Latin bullshit and get through this horrible business."

Raul kept his smile, now fueled by the intensity of the battle over the Don Salazarios that had raged overnight between his sentimentality and his conscience. He knew

Gessleman would pay him the money. But that was no longer enough. His amigos were right. The Don Salazarios belonged to him. They were his birthright. *I will slice this ripe casaba,* he thought. *I will tease out its succulent fruit—in this case, money* and *my grandfather's cigars.*

"As you wish, Señor. We should at least sit down, don't you think?" He led them to the table.

Seated, Raul leaned forward.

"Mr. Kennedy's cigars, pardon me, *your* cigars, are safely resting in Massachusetts, and they will be delivered to you there. I will arrange for their delivery just as soon as the matter of payment is concluded. As you know, there were some complications, and I must take care of certain expenses immediately. Money has a way of sealing lips that can otherwise go dangerously loose."

Wesley Cameron, twitched nervously and began to speak. "We—I—you never told us that you . . ." He stalled, his mouth working but the sentences lodged somewhere between his larynx and tongue.

Cornelius Gessleman leaned forward, glaring at his son-in-law. Then he faced Raul. "What the congressman is so eloquently trying to say is that he agreed to buy some cigars from you. That's all. There was no arrangement sanctioned by him concerning how you came by those cigars. Simple as that." His eyes left Raul's and drifted to the cigars at his elbow.

"But, Señor Gessleman," Raul began. "When Congressman Cameron agreed on your behalf to buy the *presidente*'s cigars, he knew, and *you* knew, whose cigars they were, and that the *presidente* was not making a gift of them to you. In fact, that is precisely why you desired them so. You thought the *presidente* had forced you into crime! Do you not remember saying exactly that as we smoked and talked together that night two months ago?"

Though Raul had Gessleman's full attention, he noted the old man's fingers inching toward the cigars before him.

"I am sure," Raul continued, looking at Cameron, "the congressman remembers how I explained to him that removing the cigars from the *presidente*'s home would require a diversion, like the magician's hands. One fools while the other tools."

Raul was pleased with himself at that one. It helped matters, he thought, if he kept his half of the discussion lighthearted, as if, to him, assassinating heads of state to steal their cigars was routine. It had been his earlier quip about the magician and the bunny that had blended so fortuitously with the evil in Dallas to set the stage for tonight's adventure. That his amigos had not yet found a satisfactory diversion when tragedy struck in Dallas was, for Raul, part of the morbid serendipity that had landed them here.

Gessleman, now rolling one of the cigars in front of him with a skeleton-like forefinger, looked up thoughtfully. Raul saw that Gessleman was toying with a Sancho Panza Dorados, an elegantly slender cigar distinguished by its gold foil wrapper.

"Señor Salazar," Gessleman began. *Progress,* thought Raul. *He's being diplomatic.* Raul sensed also that the combative quality had faded from Gessleman's tone. Instinctively, Raul knew that Gessleman must be at his most dangerous when he appeared calm.

"You paint a picture of complicity on the part of me

and my son-in-law in our president's death. Nothing could be further from the truth. You and I both know that. You have summoned us here because you want money. Money for silence, correct? Money in exchange for a promise, whatever *that's* worth, that this whole—" Gessleman paused, shooting another angry glare in the direction of the pale congressman—"that this whole fiasco goes quietly away somewhere, forever. The only question is how much? How rich do you and your friends think you can make yourselves because you have involved us in this criminal catastrophe? And how many hooks for how many years will be in Wesley's back as a member of the government? Isn't that about it?"

Raul settled back, doing his best to display a pensive, nonthreatening face. Then he broke into a smile, a benevolent smile born of showing generosity. It was time to play his hand. More than that, it was yet another *momento de verdad,* another pirouette and thrust with the *estoque* as he sought to bring this bull cleanly down.

"Señor Gessleman, you and the congressman are as deeply involved in the events of this month as I and my amigos. But do I wish to become rich, rich like you? No. I have riches enough for any man. I am healthy. A beautiful woman loves me. We may marry and, God willing, have children. If that happens, I will be truly rich."

Raul lifted one of the cigars from his own fan—a Ramon Allones Specially Selected Robusto—and neatly trimmed it with his grandfather's gold cutter. Rubbing the cutter for luck, Raul slipped it back into his vest pocket and lit the cigar. He gave the aroma-charged smoke a moment to rise and circulate, then continued.

"We made a bargain, your son-in-law and I. I have kept that bargain. I have secured your cigars for you, but as you can imagine, the—ah—diversion in Dallas has escalated their cost. But not, as you fear, by a fortune. No, only by, what is for you, a modest sum that will ensure the episode is closed forever."

Raul let the moment linger, drawing on his cigar, watching Gessleman's eyes. *The crafty old fox,* he thought. *He tells me nothing. Well, I will know, soon enough.*

"And what might this 'modest escalation' be?" Gessleman asked finally.

*Now,* thought Raul, *for Rosa, for us, for everything.*

"Eighty thousand dollars more," he replied with polite conviction. "A total of one hundred thousand dollars and history will never include any of us in what had to be done to get your cigars. And, of course, you get the cigars."

As he watched Gessleman's eyes, he saw them briefly reflect surprise, then relief. *No,* thought Raul. *I should not have asked for more. This whole adventure had a noble purpose: to reunite with Rosa in Cuba and see that the needs of her mountain children are met.* That portion of the one hundred thousand dollars left after paying the amigos represented Gessleman's contribution to that worthy end. There was no place for greed's contamination.

Gessleman remained silent, his face now stoic.

*That's right,* thought Raul. *You cannot let yourself show how my modest proposal has stunned you. Only, you forget, my friend, I grew up in a casino. I have watched thousands of faces at the gaming tables. I have seen masters conceal their good fortune when the cards came their way. Do you think you can bluff me? I do not think so. I will give you the time you need to play your hand because I know what you are holding—nothing, except my one hundred thousand dollars and Don Salazarios. That is all I want from you.*

Finally Gessleman spoke, his voice cold and precise. "What guarantee do we have that this will be the end of it? None. We both know that. You expect me to hand over one hundred thousand dollars tonight, and I expect to hear from you again, the next time you and your pals need money."

Raul watched Gessleman fondle the Sancho Panza. Maybe the evening was pregnant with more opportunity than he had dared hope. It was time to reach for the rest. He drew deeply on his cigar and exhaled in a long, resigned blow.

"Señor Gessleman, it comes down to trust, good will and trust. To show my good will and that you can trust my word, I will make you an offer." Raul lowered his eyes to the table.

"I see that you know the Sancho Panza brand, one of my island's finest. I still have three unopened boxes of them. After they are gone, this country will not see them, for how long?

"As it turns out there were three boxes of a brand called Don Salazario among the Kennedy cigars, an obscure brand made by my grandfather. They have sentimental value for me. My amigos who liberated the Kennedy cigars saw these and brought them back when they returned from Massachusetts. They are rightfully yours. But I am willing to trade one of these last three boxes of Sancho Panzas to you for the three boxes of Don Salazarios. You can take the box of Sancho Panzas with you tonight. Agreed?"

There. It was done. His conscience satisfied and the bait cast, all in a puff of smoke. Raul sat back, studying his quarry.

Gessleman blinked, then smiled—*an iguana's smile,* thought Raul.

"No," Gessleman said. "But here's what I *will* do. You want to show good will? Here's your chance. Three for three. Trade me the *three* boxes of Sancho Panzas for your grandfather's cigars."

Now it was Raul's turn to conceal the dealer's favor. He willed his face to stone. Then, with a reluctant sigh, he said, "Done," not believing the fresh breeze of luck that had just blown his way. "And the rest . . . ?" he ventured.

"Oh, hell. Of course," said Gessleman. "At this point, what choice do I have? Wesley, get one hundred thousand dollars out of that briefcase you're carrying and give it to Señor Salazar."

Gessleman removed a gleaming platinum device that resembled a pen from his breast pocket. He pierced the end of the now naked cigar.

"You know something, Señor Salazar?" he said quietly. "I believe we'll stay for dinner after all. It will give you time to get to know me a bit better. By the end of the evening, I believe you will appreciate that it would be *very* foolish of you to ask for any more money." Gessleman's eyes narrowed. "Foolish *and* unhealthy," he added.

Then, looking at his son-in-law, he said, "Wesley, would you quit staring and give the man his money?" He turned back to Raul and leaned close. "Another thing. You spoke of delivery. Under no circumstances are you or your *amigos* to come near my farm in Kentucky. I have a place on Cape Cod that should be convenient for you, since the cigars are still up there. I will give you instructions and will arrange to be there for their delivery. Understood?"

Raul smiled and nodded. "Perfectly, Señor Gessleman. Perfectly."

# THIRTEEN

THE FREEZING ATLANTIC chill, partially rebuffed by his plaid mackinaw, found beachheads wherever Hiram Thorpe's exposed skin surfaced. Under the padded earflap of his Maine woodsman cap, Hiram's ears burned with the snap of early winter. Thinking of Luther snugged in front of the cast-iron stove back at the office didn't help, and neither did the short Muniemaker Breva that refused to stay lit in the persistent drizzle.

Hiram stamped the sludge off his rubber boots as well as he could and entered the motel office, pausing to look toward the darkening east. No doubt about it, a storm was on its way.

Nestor Pinwood looked up from his copy of *Yankee* magazine.

"Hiram, close the damn door! Costs enough to keep this place heated without you let'n it all out."

Hiram complied, regretting he had to deal with the owner of the Gem o' the Sea at all. The motel, miles away from the tourist hubs because it was miles away from the sea, had ceased being a gem of *anything* years ago, if it ever had been one to begin with. The six weather-bleached bungalows, once a thirties "auto court," were now nothing more than a sorry enclave of low-cost housing for the transients and casual workers who filled the demand for service labor during the summer season. Pinwood kept the place open year-round simply because he lived there and had nothing else to do and nowhere else to go.

"Hello, Nestor. Haven't seen you for a while. How've you been?"

The innkeeper eyed the constable with suspicion. "All right, I guess."

This would not be easy. It never was with Nestor. Past sessions with the crotchety New Englander had confirmed Nestor was starved for company but would never admit it. There was no other explanation for the way the simplest request for information turned into a cat-and-mouse game that could span hours. Hiram usually sent Luther, who relished the game, or resigned himself to indulging the old coot.

Not today. Hiram's instincts told him the break-ins at the Hyannisport mansion were the tip of an iceberg that could catapult a local constable into a national fool. He was determined not to let that happen. Best to be prepared, and the way to do that was to gather information. Quickly.

"Been busy, Nestor?"

"Nope."

"Any customers at all this month?"

A cocked eyebrow. "Mebbe." Hiram took that as a yes.

"Couple of Spanish-looking guys? Mexican or possibly Cuban?"

Pay dirt. Too late, Nestor erased the flash of surprise.

"Don't know's I know what you mean. They all look alike to me."

"Let me help you, Nestor. One was named Pedro, tall with a thin mustache. About six foot. Another, shorter, about five feet, six inches, stocky and muscular. Called himself 'Hor-hay.' Left this area day before yesterday, probably in a hurry."

Hiram read the disappointment in Pinwood's eyes. It should have taken at least an hour to reach this point. Then he burst the bubble of illusion that there would be any game at all.

"Let's just take a look at your register," he said, reaching for the gray ledger he had pawed through several times before.

"So there were four of them," Hiram said, after scanning the pages for October and November. "And they were here a few weeks. Found work, did they? The Kennedy estate?"

Nestor Pinwood nodded, deflated.

"This Boston address—probably no good. Looks like they took two cottages. Anyone been in 'em since?"

Nestor shook his head. "Ain't even changed the beds yet," he mumbled.

"Good. Keep 'em just like that. Want to get the state boys to come over and check for prints. Should be within a day or so. I bet they paid cash, right?"

"Yep. Nice new twenty-dollar bills."

"They had just this one car?" Hiram asked, copying the Florida license number.

"Yep. An old Chevy sedan, green."

*Poor Nestor,* thought Hiram. *Now that he's lost the game, he can't wait to give away more.*

Hiram pulled out a pack of Muniemakers and ensured he had a good light before stepping out into a steady, chilling rain. The ones in the black Caddie aren't going to be this easy, he thought as he cupped the glowing cigar.

Cornelius Gessleman had used the chauffeured drive from his Palm Beach estate to solve his problem. He stepped out of the car into the brisk Kentucky evening, his head cleared of the night before. Refreshed and confident, he stretched his legs and strolled over to the white fence edging the pasture nearest the manor house. The solution was so simple, as he had known it would be.

He now owned the Kennedy cigars, or at least most of them, and was pleased with himself for having bested his host. Securing three boxes of coveted Sancho Panzas in exchange for those obscure Don something or others confirmed the old panther still had a bite.

*What a rube,* thought Gessleman as he reached across the fence and scratched the muzzle of Glo-bug, his candidate in the coming year's Triple Crown. Recalling Raul Salazar's smiling hospitality, he told the blowing horse, "Fella thinks that front he put up fooled me. 'Good will.' 'Trust.' Ha! Conniving hustler plans to be in my pocket the rest of my life. Not so, my fine one, not so."

Cornelius cradled the horse's nose and savored the brush of silky hair against his cheek. Energy from the animal throbbed across the fence, affirming his decision.

*It has always been this way,* he thought. *The courage to act has been my strength. It has separated me from the others. It's what took a small family business and turned it into a fortune. I can't let this Cuban extortionist and that incompetent dolt my daughter married destroy all I've built.*

"Oh, yes, yes, yes." He laughed aloud, as the horse tousled and blew some more.

Gessleman sighted down the unbroken line of sparkling fence. *When the boards are rotten or weak, we rip them out. That's what I'm doing, removing something rotten and something weak, that's all. Get this whole sorry business behind me. Too bad about Margie. But she's still young and pretty enough. Maybe next time— who knows?*

*As for the Cuban,* he thought, *this will be poetic justice. The blackmailing assassin will get what he deserves. Just as soon as he's delivered the cigars.* He peeled the foil from another Sancho Panza and walked, humming, toward the house.

Later, in his study, pleased with the even burn of the magnificent cigar, Cornelius Gessleman opened a locked desk drawer and removed a black leather notebook. It had no markings. He riffed its pages with purpose, knowing exactly where to stop.

"Ah, yes." He spread the book open to read the number and the coded greeting that would identify him. "Marinara," he chuckled. Then he remembered. With all the Don had been into, he loved his food. He dialed and sat back, listening, wondering if he would still recognize the voice.

# FOURTEEN

JOSEPH BONAFACCIO JR. stepped from the elevator, bowed, and swept his arm toward the hallway's brocaded expanse. "This way, Laurie-May," he cooed to the lithe blonde.

Her eyes widened in happy reaction to the rich decor of the twenty-fourth-story entry to Joseph Bonafaccio's legendary playpen apartment.

A slender Rafael Gonzalez Lonsdale clamped in his teeth, Joseph extended both arms to the leggy Rockette and proceeded to waltz her across the carpet, grazing rococo statues of cupids and plump nudes with his topcoat. Laurie-May's promising laughter reached a delighted crescendo as they reached the ornately decorated penthouse door, breathless and clinging together.

"Hey! You really *can* dance!" Joseph laughed. He opened the door, his back to the apartment, and prepared to sweep her inside. Her startled look stopped him. He spun around, smack into a frowning Dominick Romelli.

"Caesar Romero!" Laurie-May squealed, staring down at Romelli.

"Dom. What's up? Thought you'd be asleep hours ago." Joseph cocked his head in the direction of Romelli's adjoining apartment down the hall, hoping he'd take the hint.

"Uh, Joseph, I hate to interrupt your evening but something's come up. We need to talk."

When his father's surrogate needed to talk, Joseph listened.

"Sure, Dominick." He turned to Laurie-May, who was fishing in her purse. "Sweetheart, I need to spend a few minutes here with Dominick. I'll get you a glass of bubbly and you can sit and enjoy the view. I won't be long, okay?"

He turned back to see Romelli shaking his head. "Joseph, I think that you might want to postpone things with the young lady. We might be going away on business."

Joseph studied Romelli for a few seconds. Then he turned and faced Laurie-May. She was fluttering a small loose-leaf notebook. "Before I go," she asked coyly, "could I get Mr. Romero's autograph?"

Joseph and Romelli watched from the doorway as Laurie-May stepped into the elevator and gave a jaunty wave before she disappeared. Joseph sighed and closed the door.

"You don't know, Dom, how much I was looking forward to peeling off those mesh stockings. It's taken two weeks to get her up here. Jesus!"

Joseph led the way into the paneled library alcove and draped himself across one of two wing-backed leather chairs positioned opposite each other at a marble table. Romelli sat in the other.

Discarding the Rafael Gonzalez, now a symbol of the failed evening, Joseph opened the burled humidor on the table. After lighting an H. Uppman Connoisseur No. 1 Robusto, his favorite cigar for moments of stress or intense concentration, he asked, "Okay, what's up?"

Romelli leaned forward, his voice low.

"I got a call earlier tonight. A 'Marinara' call."

Joseph stiffened. The "Marinara" code had fallen out of use before the Don died. Employed to identify people designated by the Don as entitled to benefit by the unique solutions he could provide for their problems, the system had simply faded away as the family and its business changed. Joseph had known, but never asked, about the ledger Romelli used to keep, listing those who held "Marinara" privileges. He had assumed it had been destroyed.

"You, ah, checked it out?" Joseph asked.

Romelli nodded. "Yeah, he's entitled," he said. "I remember the guy. The Don used to do business with him: textiles, cotton, tobacco, and stuff.

"There was this time your father had to move some goods in a hurry and this guy helped him by taking them off his hands at a good price and mixing them in with his own. The Don was very appreciative. He introduced me to the guy and gave him 'Marinara' status as well as this phone number. The Don made me promise to help the guy out if he ever called, no matter what he wanted, know what I mean?"

Joseph nodded. Old business. The kind of stuff that drew on Dominick Romelli's craftsmanship as a skilled hit man. Not just sloppy jobs with a stubby, mean pistol or the random mess of a tommy gun, but long-range stuff requiring the intricate tools and concentration of the sniper. In the early days, as Joseph Senior built and consolidated his empire, it was occasionally necessary for his father to use terminal persuasion. Anonymous terror became a Bonafaccio trademark.

Joseph felt a surge of adrenaline as he considered Romelli's story. He imagined how his father must have felt when he dispensed death sentences as favors. The power, the . . .

"Joseph?"

"What? Oh, hell, Dom, just thinking. Tell me, how does this justify blowing up my night with Laurie-May? I don't really know how these things were handled between you and the Don, so correct me if I'm wrong. When you used to get a contract, wasn't that between you and whoever hired you? I mean, if it was family business, it was part of your job, I know that. Like the Victor Salazar thing. But for something like this, didn't you used to just make your own deal?"

Romelli hunched farther forward, frowning. He had never really trusted the elaborate security safeguards installed at the penthouse. He had preached to Joseph the necessity of assuming all offices and phones were bugged.

"Joseph, we can discuss my arrangements with 'clients' later. There's a good reason I pulled the curtain on your evening with 'Glory-day,' or whatever her name was."

Joseph drew on his cigar, waiting.

"Well," Romelli continued, "this guy has a job that needs doing, two jobs actually. Real wet work. I told him I was pretty much out of play these days, but that I would think it over. He's offering one hundred thousand dollars per. I told him I would need to know who the subjects were, you know, make sure there would be no conflicts of interest. That's when things got interesting."

Joseph puffed on the Uppman, his head back and eyes closed. Inside, the adrenaline still churned. So much like his father to have made a commitment like that. God, what days those must have been! Not surrounded by a bunch of accountants and lawyers. Just good men like Dominick Romelli, who knew the *real* ins and outs of the business.

"Joseph, one of the guys he wants taken out is our old friend Raul Salazar. We were just talking about him last night, remember?"

Joseph Bonafaccio shot forward. Coincidence in this part of his business, the part involving the old days, was rare, so rare as to be no coincidence. He stood up, his mind racing.

"You were right to interrupt, Dom. Victor Salazar makes three million dollars of our money disappear, and eight years later diamonds start falling out of his family's cigars. Now someone wants to take out Victor's son."

Joseph crossed to the picture window and looked out over the park and the city lights. Always, when he had to think something through, he stood there, feeling the power of one mind above the anonymous thousands. He knew what he had to do.

"Dominick, the softest thing the Don ever did was let Raul Salazar out of Cuba. There's *got* to be a connection. Get a couple of guys, you know, specialists. Let's go visit Señor Salazar and smoke some of his cigars."

Romelli frowned. "Specialists? You mean . . . ?"

Joseph pressed the glowing point of the Uppman into the ash tray, smashing the life out of it. Raul Salazar could well be the key to the three-million-dollar puzzle the Don had never solved. Now it was his turn.

"Yeah, specialists. Guys that can make someone talk. There's some business that the lawyers and accountants just can't handle."

# FIFTEEN

THE THIN BRASS nail surrendered to Raul's gentle pressure with the silver pry, breaking the seal of the embossed cedar box. A row of tan Don Salazario Presidentes greeted him, each ringed by a silk band bearing his grandfather's *marque.*

When Cornelius Gessleman duped himself and surrendered the Don Salazarios in favor of the Sancho Panzas, Raul's conscience was satisfied. That one man's greed could become another man's salvation seemed, to Raul, the theme of the cosmic vapor in which this whole adventure was unfolding.

Raul's mission achieved—Gessleman's payment—the honest acquisition of three perfectly sealed boxes of his grandfather's craft seemed to further dress the whole enterprise in a noble mantle. That the Don Salazarios had come to Raul through burglary and theft was refined in the complex smelter of his conscience. After all, the president's brief ownership of the cigars had not rested on an immaculate foundation. As far as Raul was concerned, the Don Salazarios were a perfect fit into the equation of reuniting his life with Rosa's. He now had two boxes of the precious cigars they would share to honor special occasions in the years ahead, and a box to one day pass on to their son.

Raul lifted the lid, closed his eyes, and let his olfactory senses transport him back to his youth in the Vuelta Abajo. Whoever had cared for these cigars before the unfortunate president had done well. They were perfectly aged and appeared as fresh as the day his grandfather had carefully laid them in the hand-crafted box.

That these particular cigars had been rolled by his grandfather, he had no doubt. He was delighted to find the old man's signature striped silk ribbon, scarlet and orange, encircling the first cigar. Raul gently lifted its folded ends, raising the cigar and freeing the others.

He removed four cigars and slipped them into a leather pocket case, which he laid on the pine table in the center of the room. Then he closed the lid of the box and tapped the nail closed with the small hammer of the pry tool.

He carried the box to the locked humidor room adjoining the wine cellar below Noches Cubanas, let himself in, and placed the resecured box on top of its two companions. Picking up the leather case as he left the cellar, he slipped it into the breast pocket of his jacket and went upstairs to pack.

*One for each of us,* he thought, as he folded clothes into his suitcase. *Before and after we make love.* Maybe now, with my gift and with news of my plan, she will say yes again and we will finally marry. Perhaps the cigars will help us have a son. If she says no, well, we will have enjoyed four magnificent cigars. *She will say yes,* he told himself.

On one wall of his office hung a large framed photograph of Raul on the flying bridge of *Don Salazario,* his marlin-rigged fishing boat. Next to it hung a framed original poster of Manolete. The matador was portrayed elegantly, head down, as the twisting head of an enraged bull sought its tormentor in vain.

Raul swung the poster aside and opened the wall safe it concealed. He removed a pile of bills and counted them one last time: sixty thousand dollars. This was his gift to Rosa after paying each of the amigos ten thousand dollars. Only a start, true, considering what was needed. But it *was* a start. Maybe now she would believe him. He was ready to return home.

Raul patted his coat pocket. The ticket for Kingston was there, right next to the cigars. There was one thing to do before he left.

"Paulo. Come and sit with me a minute. We must talk before I leave."

The tall maître d' followed, and they sat at the end of the empty bar, their usual place of business.

"You will be gone how long, Raul, three days?" asked Paulo.

"Yes, three days, I think. It depends. We may have something to celebrate, Rosa and I. If so, I will try my hardest to persuade her to stay longer, maybe a week. I will call you and let you know. But there is something else. Something I must share with you. You may decide when to tell the others."

Paulo smiled. "I already know, Raul. You are an open book sometimes. I see it in your eyes and all around us; you, the restaurant, it is all coming to an end, no? You will again ask Rosa to marry you and she will accept. Only this time you will not be leaving your home—you will be returning to it. Am I not right?"

Raul crooked his arm tightly around his friend's neck. "Yes. Yes, you are right." He laughed. He met and held Paulo's gaze.

"Paulo, come with me. After I sell the restaurant, we will do it again, in Havana or Varadero. Rosa will have her clinic; I will have my Rosa. But I am not a nurse. I, like you, am a host. I bring people hospitality. It is in my blood.

"These Yankees are crazy to turn their backs on Cuba, but the rest of the world still loves our beautiful beaches, our people, our gorgeous women, our cigars. The Norte Americanos could have had the friendship of our wonderful country. Maybe even the fifty-first state, no?" They both laughed.

"Well, maybe not a state, but a partner, a playful child, better even than it was before the revolution. Cuba needed the revolution, and America needs friends to the south. They are being so stupid. But for people like you and me, people who know and love graciousness, style, good food, wine, cigars—the rest of the world will seek us out.

"Think on it, Paulo. Come with me and be my partner. Fifty-fifty. The third Noches Cubanas: Raul Salazar and Paulo Enriquez, proprietors. You have served my father and me so well these many years, you deserve that. Give me your answer when I return."

Raul grasped Paulo's shoulder and shook it playfully. "Ah! Look at you. Tears of joy, I hope. And listen to me. Full of proposals. To you, and to Rosa. Wish me luck."

They stood and hugged, Paulo struggling for words.

"Do not speak, my friend," Raul said. "I know what your answer will be and my heart sings. Adios."

# SIXTEEN

CHUCKLING, NESTOR PINWOOD hung up the phone.

*Smartass constable. Thought he was pretty slick the other day gett'n the jump on me about those Mexicans. Oh, he was quick all right, figurin' out they took two cottages and trickin' it out of me so fast about their car and all. But he'll learn. Oh yes, he will. Got to do these things right. Got to be civil and take time to talk to people if you want to really learn somethin'. Hell, I would've told him about the third cottage and the one hundred dollars extra them fellas paid me to store their boxes in there. Might still, if he ever asks. Now, wonder if I should call him and tell him that fella "Hor-hay" just called and said they're on their way up to pick up their boxes? Or should I just wait and make him do his job?*

Pedro Vasquez had been many things in his life. Car thief, trumpeter, cigar roller, burglar, chef, and sometimes bookmaker. But he had never been in love, really in love. Until now.

The scent of crushed rose petals, the flash of her indigo eyes, the smile that drew him into her soul. Everything that was Felicia Mercado haunted him.

When Raul had summoned Pedro and Jorgé to give them instructions about delivering the cigars to the rich Americano, Pedro's heart had skipped with a rare lightness. Finally, an opportunity to put right his base mistreatment of this angel.

Pedro had penned four letters of contrition, four collections of failed words. He had crumpled and discarded each of them. But now, with his eyes and hands, he would *tell* her, *show* her, what was in his heart.

"I'll drive, Jorgé," Pedro said, as they approached Raul's 1960 Pontiac Bonneville Coupe. Jorgé laughed, tossing him the keys. "Cousin, why is it I think we are about to set a south-to-north speed record? Let me know when you are tired. I promise you, I will keep up the pace."

# SEVENTEEN

THE CARIBBEAN SHIMMERED below, a translucent azure sheet, blanketing stippled coral reefs that sprouted from a white, sandy floor. *Soon, my darling,* Raul thought, *soon.* He cinched his seat belt as the Jamaica Air DC-3 banked and settled onto its final approach to Kingston.

Raul saw her as he stepped from the airplane door to the top of the wheeled stairs. Rosa was next to the terminal door, her flower-print skirt fluttering in the light breeze, her skin a golden glow against the white stucco building. Raul bolted the stairs and ran to her.

"Rosa, Rosa, my precious Rosa. I have missed you so much!" He smothered her in his arms.

Holding her away, a hand on each bare shoulder, he fed his starved senses. There had been too many partings in the past eight years. He had learned to draw on these moments of greeting as warming currency against future bankrupt loneliness. Then he stiffened and folded his arms.

"This does not look like the uniform of a revolution-ary nurse!" he said with mock sternness, taking in the vibrant colors of her dress.

"And you do not look like a cigar thief," she giggled. "For now, for *you,* I am revolting *against* the revolution." Then, biting his ear, she whispered, "Come, we will make our own revolution. Many bullets will be fired, yes? I have already checked us into the hotel. Let us go; the uprising has started."

Raul slipped off the light linen blazer when he entered the hotel room. As he did, the leather cigar case fell to the floor. He stooped to pick it up and rose to see Rosa step-ping out of her flowered skirt. Her exquisite molting made him catch his breath.

"Ah, Rosa!" he exclaimed, torn between what he had planned and what was happening.

"I have brought something with me," he stammered, awkwardly fumbling with the leather case. "A very special way to celebrate our reunion. Something to share before we make love and before I show you my surprise."

His eyes roamed her again. "But it will wait." He laughed, laying the case on the bedside table and hastening with his belt.

"Or maybe it will not," she retorted, snatching the case. She pulled a towel from the bathroom and demurely covered herself.

"In Miami, those many miles of ocean from me, you

are able to generously plan the time you will take before we make love. Now, here, you are not so patient. Let me see what you thought we would share before we shared each other. It must be *very* important!"

Aware he had lost a small battle, Raul sheepishly watched her open the cigar case. She stood away, her eyebrows arched.

"Cigars," he admitted, "Don Salazarios. One for each of us, before and after. I thought they . . ." He could not explain the romantic impulse that had possessed him in Miami.

"Oh, so my brave Fidel would rather smoke a cigar than make love to his precious Rosa!" she cajoled, squirming and letting the towel fall. "You know, Fidel, how much I love cigars, but I like to choose them myself!"

She tossed the case aside, pushed him onto the bed and slid off his shoes, followed by his pants and shorts. Then, dropping alongside his hip, she took his swelling rise in her hand. Studying it, she brushed aside the dark pendant of curls dangling from her head and said softly, "Now, *this* is a perfect cigar, a robusto, at least a fifty-four, no? This is the cigar I wish to smoke first." Raul moaned with pleasure as he watched himself disappear into her smile, her eyes locked on his.

They filled the afternoon making love as they never had before. She, anticipating and hoping; he, knowing and teasing; both became lost in unexplored excitements that led them to even higher peaks. Finally, spent and glistening, they napped in each other's arms.

Later, leaning against the railing of the tiled deck, they

sipped rum and tonics and let the Caribbean evening wrap them in the richness of Calypso and warm offshore breezes.

"And now, my hero," Rosa purred, stroking his disheveled curls, "while my favorite cigar is resting, we can smoke one of those others while you tell me of your surprise."

Smiling, Raul went back into the room. She had been right. Their lovemaking, at first a frantic, spending conflagration, then exquisitely tarried, had cocooned him in a surround of sensual enchantment well matched to the rich pleasure of a Don Salazario. The mood and the setting were perfect for the rest. First, the cigars.

He brought out a folded brown bag from his suitcase and set it on the patio's glass table. Then he drew one of the Don Salazarios from the case, cut it cleanly, and lit it with a thick wooden match. Satisfied of an even light, he handed her the glowing cigar and prepared one in the same manner for himself.

They sat and smoked for a while, as steel drums hammered out a distant rhythm. *It is time,* he thought.

"Rosa, the rich old man's greed cost him more than the twenty thousand dollars we'd planned on. After Kennedy's assassination, an opportunity suddenly appeared and I took it. Now, instead of just a few thousand dollars for the clinic, there is enough to change everything, for you, the clinic, and for us."

Watching the question in her eyes grow, he reached into the paper bag and drew out a pile of bills. Then another and another.

Grinning, he spilled the entire contents on the table. "Sixty thousand. Enough to rebuild the clinic, to buy medicine, supplies. For whatever is needed."

He stopped and took a long draw on the cigar, reveling in her expression of disbelief.

"How . . . ? From where does this . . . ?"

Raul laughed. Never had he seen this woman of action, of strength, so speechless.

"It is a long, long story. One that we can tell our children and grandchildren someday."

Her wide eyes searched his in silence.

"Yes, Rosa. I want to come home. I am again asking you to marry me. I, too, want to be a revolutionary." He grinned. "Will you have me? Will Fidel?"

Her robe flew apart as she leaped to her feet. Laughing and crying at the same time, she threw her arms around him, sending the billowing terry cloth in a sweeping arc. It brushed her Don Salazario and sent it rolling. The cigar disappeared over the edge of the table.

"Raul, oh Raul, I am so happy. Yes, I will have you. I do not know about Fidel. Maybe he will be too jealous to allow such a handsome man on his island. But for me, yes, yes, and yes. Is it true? Can we finally be together forever?"

"Yes, my love, we can. Sit down. I will explain."

He reached down to retrieve the Don Salazario from the tile floor. As his fingers touched the cigar, something caught his eye—something in the long ash that had powdered in its gentle collision with the tile, something that gleamed with a tantalizing brightness. He trapped the glittering object in his fingers and held it up against the luminous moon. There, bare and exposed, he saw what it was.

"*Madre de Dios!*" he whispered, the impact of his father's terrible last words to him crashing through time.

"*Look for some of your grandfather's cigars . . . I will send them to our old friend, Paulo . . . Enjoy the cigars, and remember me.*"

# EIGHTEEN

"CONSTABLE, THE FAMILY is simply not interested in pursuing this. That's all there is to it. As far as they are concerned, there were no break-ins, there was no theft—of cigars or anything else. The matter is closed. Under the circumstances, I am sure you understand."

Hiram Thorpe held the telephone receiver away and stared at it in disbelief. The president had been assassinated. The country was ablaze with rumors and news probes of conspiracy. Within hours of the assassination, there had been at least one, perhaps *two*, break-ins and a theft at the Kennedy estate. On *his* watch! And this toad was now telling him the burglaries never happened. Slowly, Hiram brought the receiver back to his ear.

"Well, son, I'll tell you. I've got two documented break-ins at the place within, oh, say, twelve hours. I've got four suspicious Latin types hanging around here a couple of weeks, two of 'em working at the place and a third breaking the heart of a sweet little chambermaid who didn't know any better. Two days before the first break-in, she showed him the room that a week ago was full of cigars and now doesn't have a one. And I've got a sighting of some goons speeding out of town after the second break-in.

"Now that's a hell of a lot of criminal activity going on in my backyard. Your sayin' it didn't happen doesn't change the fact that it did."

Hiram began patting his pockets in search of a Muniemaker.

"I respect the Family's need for privacy during this time; but, son, there's a crime been committed up here. Hell, two or three crimes, maybe more. Who knows what it means? Sooner or later the big boys, the feds and all, are going to come snooping around wonderin'—like I'm doin'—how it all ties in with Dallas. I'm not about to tell 'em nothin' happened when it's plain as Mary Jane that somethin' did. Know what I mean?"

Hiram heard a sigh.

"Constable, I don't quite know how to put this, but try and follow. All right?

"I am positive, repeat, positive, that there will be no, ah, higher official inquiry into the, ah, alleged intrusion at the family estate. Frankly, the Family is not particularly sure of the circumstances surrounding how and when Mr. Kennedy came by some of his cigars. As far as the government *and* the Family are concerned, this is a—a dead issue. I implore you to treat it in the same fashion."

Hiram had never been "implored" before. Whatever it was, he didn't think he liked it.

"Son, there was nothing 'alleged' about those torn-up

doors. And someone just implored the shit out of that big brass lock with a hacksaw. I call that burglary and theft. 'Cording to sweet young Felicia, she helped you and some movie star carry thirty or forty boxes of cigars into that wine room back in July. Not a sign of 'em there now. You tellin' me your ex-boss smoked 'em all? Don't think so. Nope, I just don't think so."

Hiram located a Muniemaker and rolled it between his thumb and forefinger, anticipating an end to the conversation and the beginning of the smoke he was going to enjoy driving out to the Gem o' the Sea.

"I suppose," he continued, "that you're cleanin' out your desk to make room for whoever LBJ plans to put there. So tomorrow—if not already—you're history. But me, I'm going to be right here doin' my job, and I plan to keep doin' it till the voters of this county find someone who can do it better, which isn't very likely."

Hiram shot a look at Luther in the outer office, his face buried in a model airplane magazine.

"I've got an investigation to finish, and that's just what I intend to do. Be seein' you. *Maybe.*" Hiram hung up and slipped on his jacket.

"Now, Nestor," Hiram began slowly. "You called *me*, remember? I could stand here and tell you things that have been going on in the village, which ain't been much, or you could just get to the point. Maybe then, we could have a smoke and play a few hands of gin rummy. I'll make the time this morning. What do you say?"

Hiram extracted a package of Swisher Sweets from his jacket pocket and laid them on the counter. *Time to get down and dirty,* he thought, relying on Nestor Pinwood's two greatest passions as persuasion.

He left two hours later, his breath heavy with the syrup of the Swishers and his pocket $1.90 lighter. But Nestor had shown him the inside of the third cottage. Now he had a plan.

As he pulled onto the roadway, Hiram Thorpe considered whether he would put the $1.90 on his expense report.

# NINETEEN

AT SIXTY-ONE, PAULO Enriquez had settled into a resigned depression that his days would end in Miami and
he would never see Cuba again. The combined corruption
of Batista and the Mafia had so sickened Paulo that he
had reluctantly left Victor Salazar and Noches Cubanas a
year before the Bonafaccios murdered his former employer. When Raul had shown up in Miami, seeking to
start a small restaurant bearing the name of his father's
Havana establishment, Paulo had been reborn. Greeting
the world at Victor's Noches Cubanas as its chief maître
d' had been his whole life.

By the time Castro had swept away the pleasure pal-
aces and scrubbed his homeland clean of the Mafia, Paulo
had another life, in Miami's Little Havana—with Raul
and his restaurant. But Miami was not Havana.

Yes, he would return home with Raul. Cuba needed
him and many more like him. The revolutionary wind, for

now a frenetic hurricane of change, would spend itself in time. Then the real work would begin: the work of rebuilding and living instead of dreaming.

To Paulo, all governments suffered a common flaw. Inevitably, they forgot about the people they were supposed to serve and protect. A scant three years after Cuba was shed of her dictator, her savior was busy quelling the voices *he* did not want to hear. Maybe, in years to come, these growing pains would ease and the irrepressible Cuban people would again emerge, cleansed of the corruption and excess of the Batista years and seasoned by Castro's revolutionary stew. If so, Paulo wanted to be there for that glorious reawakening.

He slid from the stool and smiled at himself in the mirror behind the bar as he smoothed his peppered mustache, straightened his tie, and prepared to open the restaurant. Ah, such lofty thoughts! *But we will see,* he mused. *Raul and his Rosa; Paulo and . . . Who knows? Maybe Rosa has a cousin or even an aunt.* At his age, he could not be too choosy.

The phone rang. A reservation, he hoped. There were only four on the book that night.

"Good afternoon, Noches Cubanas," he spoke, the richly modulated greeting flowing automatically.

"Paulo! A miracle has happened! Not only will we return to Cuba as partners, we will be covered with the glory of matadors! The gangsters may have murdered my father, but his treasure is alive, ready to serve our people. I am returning to Miami in the morning. My plane leaves here at nine and arrives there at ten.

"Now, listen carefully and do *exactly* as I say. Others who would keep Victor's treasure from us may discover what I have found. We must act quickly to protect it."

Paulo stood at the bar, tense with expectation. "Yes, Raul, go ahead. I am listening."

The old Cuban's eyes widened as he absorbed his employer's words. So, he would be a revolutionary hero after all.

Paulo returned four hours later. It was eight-thirty and four men were just entering the restaurant. His heart skipped when he saw them and he was scarcely able to conceal the alarm of recognition behind the façade of his greeting.

"Good evening, gentlemen. A table for four? Right this way."

He slid four menus and a wine list from the maître d's pedestal and began to lead them into the dining room. A painful clamp on his upper arm arrested him.

"Hold on there, Mr. P. Where's the boss?"

Paulo spun around and flashed a weak smile at the wolfish grin of Joseph Bonafaccio Jr., the only person who had ever called him "Mr. P."

"Señor Bonafaccio! And Señor Romelli. What a great pleasure to see you again."

*Mierda,* he thought, trembling as Romelli released his vice grip. Raul was right to have called ahead. These hombres are not here for dinner.

"So, Mr. P., you didn't recognize me." Bonafaccio patted his stomach. "I haven't gained that much in eight years, have I?"

Paulo looked down.

"Yeah, better you don't answer that one." Bonafaccio laughed. "Look, it's good to see you. You look great. Now I'd really like to have a little talk with Raul Salazar. Where is he?"

Paulo was grateful he had something to answer honestly. He was certain there would be more to come that would require all the guile he could manage.

"Señor Salazar is out of the country. Away on a short vacation—with a lovely señorita, I think." Paulo smiled and winked.

"Well, that's good for him, bad for us. Sorry to have missed him. I brought Mr. Romelli and our associates all the way down here to meet him and have a smoke together. I hear he still has some really fine Cubans, even some pre-Castros. I was hoping to add to my collection."

Paulo smoothed his sleeve, a pretext to rub his arm and restore the circulation cut off by Romelli's clasp. He set the menus and wine list back on the shelf, hoping to discourage Bonafaccio from staying.

"As I said, he is not here, Señor."

"No," said Bonafaccio, his voice now thick and malevolent. "But *you* are. Tell you what. In light of our past relationship, I'm sure your boss would want us to see his cigar collection. Suppose you just take us to it." He poked his head around the draped entrance into the sparsely populated dining room and shook his head. "Not much for you to do in there anyway."

The grip again, gentler this time, more a guide than a threat. "Bet we're going downstairs, right?" Romelli asked softly.

# TWENTY

OFFSHORE CLOUDS, DARK with the promise of storm, muscled themselves into a ragged, low formation all along the coast. Cornelius Gessleman watched the brooding sky build through the chauffeured sedan's rear window.

"Takes something pretty damned important to get me up here this time of year," he said to his son-in-law, seated next to him. The congressman had tried to beg off, claiming important business back home in his district. Gessleman wouldn't hear of it. "You wanted these cigars so bad, you can goddamn well help me pick them up," he had said. "Who knows what that Cuban extortionist might have cooked up. Better there are two of us."

Gessleman winced as lightning flashed in the distance. "I suppose these cigars are worth it, in some crazy, historical kind of way," he said. "Now that you got the president killed over them, it would be a waste to just leave them for Salazar. Don't kid yourself though. That one hundred thousand dollars is just the beginning."

Gessleman paused, reflecting on his conversation with Dominick Romelli. That there would be no further payments to Raul Salazar he was now certain. And the other task he had discussed with Romelli . . .

"What the hell, my boy, it's an adventure." He laughed, slapping Wesley's leg. *Hell,* Cornelius thought, *it's easy to be nice to him now. I'll almost miss him—almost.*

The sandy hillocks of Barnstable County rolled by as they bore down the expressway toward South Yarmouth.

"Wake up, Luther. Company's coming." Hiram Thorpe nudged the sleeping deputy and set the half-smoked Muniemaker in the ashtray of his Dodge Dart. For this evening's work, Hiram had filled the tank of his personal car, leaving the cruiser at the office.

Luther roused and the two of them watched, shielded by the forested slope behind the Gem o' the Sea.

A red Bonneville stopped at the office and two men stepped out. The driver stretched his legs as the passenger went into the office.

*Come on now, Nestor,* Hiram thought. *Don't go getting babbly on me. Just give him the key.*

A few seconds later, the passenger emerged from the office, looked around, and walked toward the cottage. He motioned over his shoulder and the Pontiac crept along behind him, its tires lightly crunching along the carpet of dead leaves. It stopped in front of the cottage, and the driver again appeared. He opened the trunk and stood talking a moment with the other.

Through his binoculars, Hiram made out the dark-complected features of the two men. The driver, tall and muscular, with angular good looks, had to be Felicia's Pedro. The other, shorter and thin, had to be the one Nestor called "Hor-hay," though, by now Hiram knew from the fingerprint check that his name was "Jorgé Nunez." Of the four sets of prints left in the cottages, only Jorgé's had led to a criminal record, a misdemeanor conviction in Florida for racetrack touting.

The low storm clouds swallowed the scene in shadow. *No matter*, thought Hiram. *I can see all I need to*. He watched the two men go inside and reappear, carrying tiers of small boxes. After several trips they were done.

"What you suppose they're doin, Hiram?" asked Luther. "We going to take 'em in now?"

Hiram shook his head. "Nope. That's why I filled this thing with gas. We're just going to follow these boys. All the way to Miami if we have to. Don't think it's likely to come to that, though. If they had wanted to take those cigars to Miami, they could have done that the night they stole 'em. More likely, this was some kind of temporary storage. We'll just let 'em lead us to wherever those cigars are goin'. Should be kind of interesting, though no one seems to care 'cept me."

Hiram waited as the Bonneville moved slowly back to the office. Then he let his car coast down the back road and braked to a stop at the highway intersection a few yards from Gem o' the Sea. He waited ten seconds after the Bonneville pulled onto the highway before starting his engine and falling in behind it.

Twenty minutes later, the Bonneville slowed as though the driver were searching for an address. But there were no addresses, simply wrought iron gates guarding the grounds of a series of discreetly shielded estates.

"That figures," Hiram muttered, passing the Pontiac and keeping it in his rearview mirror.

"They're going to visit one of the summer residents," he said to Luther, referring to the handful of people who occupied the Cape's lavish spreads for a month or two each summer, then chased the sun on to the Bahamas or the south of France.

Hiram let the distance widen, then fill with two other cars that had also passed the Bonneville, which was now crawling along the shoulder. Just as he considered doubling back, the Pontiac turned in.

"The Gessleman place," he said. "Of course."

Hiram now recalled the article in the local paper five years earlier, just after Cornelius Gessleman had purchased the place from the heirs of an automobile tycoon. What had caught his eye at the time was the fact that he, Hiram Thorpe, a constable in rural New England, shared a passion with someone like Cornelius Gessleman, reported to be one of the five hundred wealthiest men in the country.

Though Hiram's tastes, constricted by his wallet, favored Swisher Sweets, Muniemakers, and an occasional White Owl New Yorker, he had bonded at an elemental level with this rich man he did not know, whose collection of vintage Cuban cigars had been the centerpiece of the article. To Hiram, a cigar was a cigar. Whether it cost twenty cents or twenty dollars, the moments of pleasure, contentment, and escape it furnished must be basically the same. *Still,* he had thought, *it would be nice to try one of*

*those Cubans, just once. See what all the fuss is about.*
When the embargo came, he forgot about it.

"Look alive, Luther, we're goin' in," Hiram said. He
made a U-turn across the opposite lanes and headed back.

Hiram knew the place well. During the off-season he
made it a point to swing into the grounds of the various
homes on a random basis as a visual deterrent to anyone
who might consider a little private excursion. The Kennedy place had been the exception. Once the senator had
been elected president, the feds had made it clear the local
constable was neither needed nor wanted. One reason for
his current obsession with the break-ins was his certainty
that they would not have occurred had his sporadic pa-
trols been permitted to continue.

And, of course, there had been the cigars. Since Felicia
Mercado described what she had helped carry into the
wine cellar, Hiram's curiosity had become insatiable.
There were just too many loose ends. Now, by God, he
was going to get some answers.

He parked just inside the massive gate, still open after
the Bonneville passed through. Above, iron cherubs and
sylphs danced against the blackening sky.

"Come on, Luther. Let's take a walk," he said, quietly
opening his door.

With Hiram leading, they crept along the trees lining
the circular driveway. As they made their way farther into
the property and rounded a curve, the grounds opened to
reveal the mansard wings of a sprawling chateau.

"Quite a place, huh, Luther?" Hiram whispered.
"Look in front."

The Bonneville, its trunk open, was parked behind a large Chrysler sedan. Two men were talking, while one of two others hunched over the open trunk, handing out small boxes.

"Let's hustle, Luther. Like the books say, this looks to be in 'flagrante delicto.' " Luther cocked his head, confused.

"It means catchin' 'em red-handed, Luther. Come on!"

Hiram sprinted the remaining few yards, holding his Sam Browne belt to quiet the jiggling equipment. He motioned for Luther to do the same. When they were about twenty yards away from the two cars, he stopped and unholstered his .44. Again, Luther followed suit, his eyes wide, his breath coming fast.

"Good evenin', boys," Hiram announced in a crisp, low voice. "Plan on having a smoke?"

Wesley Cameron dropped an armload of boxes onto the brick drive, shattering the silence.

Pedro and Jorgé stood frozen, their eyes taking in the uniforms and drawn weapons with what Hiram considered a practiced attitude. *These boys have been around the block,* he thought. *Should be no trouble. Just keep a sharp eye on 'em.*

The younger of the other two was fluttering like a hummingbird, scooping up the boxes he had dropped. He dropped them again, and finally stood, his arms quivering at his sides as he looked morosely at the older man.

"Wesley, would you control yourself? Officer, I am Cornelius Gessleman. This is my home. May I help you?"

Hiram studied Gessleman for several seconds. There

were three of the cigar boxes on the ground, next to the rear passenger door of the Chrysler. He leaned over and picked one of them up.

"Partagas, huh? Never tried one. Any good?"

"I hear some of them are," replied Gessleman.

Hiram set the box back down.

"And the rest," he said, sweeping his hand in the direction of the Bonneville, "know anything about them?"

Hiram let the pause that followed string out. He had deliberately thrown Gessleman a question that would force the issue. It would help him read the situation to see which way Gessleman went.

"As a matter of fact, I don't," Gessleman said at last, apparently reaching a decision.

"I, that is, we, had just come out to see what was going on. These men parked in front of my home and started taking boxes out of their car. Then, they offered them to Congressman Cameron here, my son-in-law. Very curious. I'm glad you showed up."

"Mmmm . . . ," Hiram mused. A congressman. He wasn't surprised.

"And you gents," he said turning to Jorgé and Pedro. "Care to tell me what's going on here?"

Pedro and Jorgé looked at each other a few seconds. Finally, Pedro spoke.

"Officer, my friend and I were here in your county working about a month ago. Wasn't it a month ago, Jorgé?"

Jorgé nodded in vigorous assent.

"We stayed at a motel not too far from here for several weeks, during which time we worked and enjoyed your beautiful Cape Cod. I met a lady while we were here, a lovely young señorita, and we have traveled back here so I can see her again."

Jorgé continued his nodding, a broad smile adding emphasis.

"What's that got to do with all these boxes of cigars, Mr. Vasquez?" Hiram asked, watching Pedro closely. He found no surprise in Pedro's black eyes at the use of his name by this stranger.

Pedro continued.

"Ah yes, those cigars," he smiled. "Well, Señor, when we took a room again at the motel, we found these cigars in the room. I enjoy a cigar now and then and so does Jorgé. We loaded them in our car intending to take them with us, a gift of unknown origin. Then, after we left, we started thinking. There were so many and the boxes looked so . . . so . . . expensive. We were uncomfortable with them, you know?"

No, Hiram thought. I don't know. These boys don't seem the type to stare down a gift horse. More likely, they'd saddle up and ride it away. Fast thinker, though. Got to give him credit for that. Might as well hear him out.

"So," Pedro continued, "we simply decided to leave them somewhere. We pulled into this fine home by chance, thinking that someone with a home like this would appreciate cigars like these."

As Hiram digested this Swiss cheese of a story, he began to appreciate its beauty and the wit of the man who concocted it. There was no physical evidence linking Pedro and Jorgé with the theft of Kennedy's cigars. There was simply Felicia, who showed Pedro the room where they were kept, and Nestor, who rented them the room they ended up in; circumstantially suggestive but not conclusive. With the Kennedy family denying any theft and Felicia probably reluctant to incriminate her handsome hero, there was no case.

Then Hiram thought of Felicia and smiled. This Pedro, smart and good looking, might be worthy of her. If only he were on the right side of the law.

Hiram holstered his pistol and nodded to Luther to do the same.

"So," he said to Gessleman. "You know nothing about these cigars, correct?"

"That is right, Officer. Nothing."

"And they are not your cigars, correct?"

"Most certainly, they are not."

"And you don't know these two gentlemen, correct?"

"That is correct. I do not."

Hiram smiled.

"Luther, go get my car," he said, handing Luther the keys.

As Luther disappeared down the driveway, Hiram took a seat on the base of one of the twin marble lions guarding the walkway leading to the mansion. He began patting his pockets, searching.

"Gents. Tell you what we've got here. Now I know none of you are going to believe it, but those are stolen cigars." He surveyed the shocked expressions, warming inside.

"Yep, stolen from a home here on the Cape. Now seein' as none of you claims ownership of 'em, I'm just going to have to confiscate 'em into my official custody. I'll notify the rightful owners."

Hiram's smile broadened as he anticipated *that* conversation. His thoughtful patting ceased. He pulled a pack of Swisher Sweets from his shirt pocket and held it up. "Anyone care for a cigar?" he asked.

# TWENTY-ONE

"Jesus! What a tough old bird." Joseph Bonafaccio gazed down at the Caribbean from the window of the DC-3. Romelli was seated beside him, reading *Sports Illustrated*. "What do you think, Dom? Was he telling the truth?"

Romelli gave him a patient, benevolent smile—the old master to the student.

"Joseph, it's a very hard thing to call. When a man realizes he's been so destroyed that he knows he'll die regardless of what he says, reliability is uncertain. Some finally sing, hoping, I suppose, that when it all stops, everything will be the same. Some lose the truth altogether and simply go crazy. And some decide to die with the truth locked away, their last victory. At the end, when he kept repeating he knew nothing of cigars with diamonds in 'em and that Raul Salazar was in Kingston, he had nothing further to gain or lose, you see. Or did he? That's the difficulty. It always is in these situations."

Joseph turned to the window again, reflecting.

"Well, at least we know where Salazar is. Good thing you called the hotels. He'll have a surprise from the past this morning, won't he?"

Romelli nodded and returned to his magazine. After a few seconds he closed it and stuffed it into the seat pocket. He leaned close to Bonafaccio.

"Joseph, it's tough to admit, but last night's work was too much for me. It was good we took Enzo to do it. I'll level with you; I've lost the stomach for it. It's one thing to line up crosshairs of a scope and bring something to a quick, clean end. Last night's session was something else altogether. *Capisci?*"

Joseph looked away, afraid his eyes would betray him. *He* had found the interrogation of Paulo Enriquez disturbingly thrilling. Shepherding the Bonafaccio holdings through labyrinths of tax regulations and board room strategies left him flat. But stepping back in time to the ruthless ways of his family's past had been intoxicating. This affair involving Salazar and the stolen money had fed his conviction that he should have lived in his father's time, when power rested on pillars of force and intimidation instead of columns in a ledger. He patted Romelli's arm.

"Ahh, what the hell, Dom. Victor Salazar started this in fifty-five when he turned pirate on us. His son might just be smarter. If he's got the cigars with the diamonds, maybe he'll just turn them over."

Romelli shook his head, smiling, and retrieved the *Sports Illustrated*. "Right," he said.

———

Raul tightened his arm around Rosa's shoulder as they watched the DC-3 turn off the runway and taxi toward the terminal. The bulbed silver nose of the airplane angled to the sky as if straining to return to its true element. It would be a short time on the ground, ten minutes at most. Just time enough for the arriving Miami passengers to disembark and the handful of Kingston passengers to take their place.

The whirling propellers coughed to a stop in front of the building and two attendants in shirtsleeves wheeled the portable stairway to the aircraft's oval door. Rosa looked up at Raul, tears glistening in her eyes.

"Raul, my sweet Raul. Forget all this. The money you have brought is plenty, a godsend. Return to Cuba with me now. Don't go back to Miami. The things you told me last night about your father and those monsters who killed him . . .

"If, as you think, they may discover how your father hid what he took from them, then no millions are worth that risk. Please, my love, forget this and let us finally be together."

Raul drew her close and buried her head against his shoulder. Speaking softly, he said, "Rosa, we will be together in such a short time. We have waited this long, another few days will be as nothing. So many in Cuba are being strangled by politics. These millions will make a difference.

"It will be so simple. All I have to do is collect those cigars and Paulo. I am sure he wants to return with me. I owe at least that much to the memory of my father. What he was able to take back from the gangsters belongs to our people. He paid with his life for this gift, and I must see that it is delivered."

She looked up again, her eyes clouded. His own eyes started to fill, and he looked past her to the airplane that would return him to Miami for the last time. He stiffened. *"Madre de Dios,"* he gasped.

He backed Rosa into a darkened alcove, buried his head against her shoulder, and watched through her parted hair as Joseph Bonafaccio Jr. and Dominick Romelli stepped out of his past and onto the tarmac.

# TWENTY-TWO

As the plane banked and climbed, Raul kept his eyes on the terminal until it disappeared beneath wisps of cloud.

Clasping Rosa in the shadow of the alcove, he had watched Bonafaccio and Romelli stalk briskly by, not five feet from him. Only after a waiting cab sped them from the terminal building had he given Rosa one last kiss and sprinted to the waiting plane.

Safe, for the moment, he settled back and closed his eyes. *It would be a lethal mistake to treat this as coincidence,* he thought. He smiled at the irony. The last time he had seen those two had been from the window of a climbing plane, with the lights of Havana shrinking into the night, one life ending as another began. Only then, the killers had stayed behind.

He had one hour to piece this together and improvise a solution. *Thank God for Paulo,* he thought.

———

Raul broke his race through the Miami terminal with a brief stop at a pay phone. He quickly dialed the restaurant. When there was no answer, he abandoned all pretense of blending in with other travelers and bolted for the cab line.

"Señor?" asked the driver.

"Noches Cubanas. *Arriba!* Set a record!" Raul thrust a hundred-dollar bill into the driver's hand and recoiled as the '60 Chevrolet leapt forward in a burst that numbered its transmission's days.

Ten minutes later he jumped from the cab as it slowed in front of the restaurant. Paulo's ancient pickup truck was parked in the adjacent alley. He unlocked the front door and stepped inside.

"Paulo!" His shout lost itself in the empty restaurant. Chairs were still on the floor, and the tables were bare of tablecloths. The restaurant had not been properly closed. He passed through the bar and called into the empty kitchen. Again, no answer.

Raul stood at the top of the stairs that led down to the wine cellar and humidor room. Sometimes, after a long night, his maître d' would simply sleep on the cot in the storage area outside the wine cellar.

"Paulo?" he repeated, slowly descending the stairs.

The blanket at the foot of the cot was neatly folded and the door to the wine cellar and humidor room was unlocked. He pushed it open.

The heady must of aging wine and tobacco in cedar greeted him, usually a moment of pleasure he would pause to enjoy. Not now. Another aroma greeted him, a clinging sweetness that did not belong. He reached to his right and found the light switch.

Paulo, naked and gagged, sat at the pine table in the middle of the wine cellar, his arms bound to the vertical posts of the straight-backed chair. Each of his legs was secured at the ankle by thin cord to the corresponding chair leg, forcing his hips forward and compressing his back rigidly against the slatted rise. His defeated efforts to kick out in anger or terror at the torture practiced upon him had scraped the skin from around his ankles, leaving raw streaks of blood and exposed bone.

Raul leaned against the door frame and slumped to the floor.

Gruesome objects formed two neat rows on the table in front of Paulo. From the white glints at the ends, Raul made out that some were fingers, then toes. Then a curved, small bowl of an object, an ear. Then, an indistinguishable mass, lumpy and rough. Next to it, separate and distinct, what could only be a shriveled penis. Next to that, an eye, then another.

Too numbed to scream, Raul threw up, sobbing. The grisly evidence told of his friend's slow, agonizing death. He had been forced to watch his own ghastly mutilation until he could see no more. As Raul felt consciousness rush from him, he prayed that the same mercy had been visited upon Paulo.

He woke, minutes or hours later; he was not sure. The scene had not changed. He understood completely what had happened and recognized the unmistakable signature of who had done this to Paulo. He could not call the police. He would tend to Paulo's body himself. After that, he did not know. He was shaking.

# TWENTY-THREE

RAUL WENT TO work at once. He knew he would be crippled by the waves of grief and horror washing over him if he did not stay busy. The simple mission he had hoped to accomplish was now grimly complicated, and time was running against him. He harbored no doubt that Bonafaccio knew what had become of Victor's treasure and was possessed by a savage hunger to reclaim it.

Paulo's body needed to be removed and the room cleaned before the staff arrived.

With his Bonneville off on the road trip to Cape Cod, he had only one choice for the grisly job ahead—Paulo's wreck of a pickup. He gently wrapped his friend's mutilated body, and its various parts, in the old canvas tent Paulo had used for his trips into the interior swamps. Then he hefted the ghastly bundle and carried it upstairs to the truck. All the while, images of the past flashed in his mind, scenes spinning in a dizzying collage.

His father—the Bonafaccios—his exile from Cuba—

his father's murder—Rosa's crusade—the embargo—the Kennedy cigars—the diamonds in the Don Salazarios—and, finally, this: Paulo.

Raul clamped the tailgate in place and paused a second to catch his breath. Paulo must have had time to carry out Raul's instructions before Bonafaccio showed up. The cigars had been in plain sight when Raul had left them. Now they were gone. Could Raul's brief, excited telephone call to Paulo from Kingston have been enough to ignite the will to resist such a fatally brutal interrogation? Could *any* man have buried the secret of the cigars' hiding place from such an inquisition? Then Raul recalled the look in Paulo's eyes when Raul had proposed their new venture together in Cuba. Raul had seen that look in another's eyes: Rosa's.

As the kaleidoscope spun, other fragments emerged and hovered before tumbling into place. Slowly, a picture, a *new* picture, began to form.

The cigars could wait. They would have to. The wick of fate kindled by Victor Salazar and now fueled by Bonafaccio's fierce vengeance burned rapidly toward conflagration. There was much to do and precious little time. Raul slid into the dusty cab of the pickup and set off for the deepest part of Little Havana.

Dominick Romelli pressed a fifty dollar bill into the hand of the startled desk clerk with a pressure calculated to send a clear message. Romelli's basset hound eyes capped a congenial smile as his thumb gouged the sweaty palm, sharply persuading the clerk to abandon the hotel's privacy policy.

"Sir, though Señor Salazar has not checked out and is scheduled to stay with us another three days, I saw him and the lady leave early this morning. I believe they took a cab to the airport. I have not seen them since. If, as you say, the hotel operator told you when you called earlier that he still was a guest, it is because he still appears to be. I do not know if he will be returning."

Romelli released the pressure and turned to Joseph, who shrugged and pointed his chin toward the door. As they left the hotel, Bonafaccio said, "That's it, then. He's split. Shouldn't be much of a problem to track him from the airport. Only one or two flights out of here a day, right?"

Within thirty minutes they confirmed they had crossed paths with Raul Salazar at the airport. Joseph sulked as he sat in the waiting area clutching his ticket on the 3:00 P.M. flight to Miami. One fleecing by the Salazars was one too many. He would recover the treasure skimmed from the Bonafaccio family, with interest.

# TWENTY-FOUR

THE POCKED STUCCO front of the dreary, low building revealed nothing. It was simply one of the many hundreds of wretched, though functional, structures in Little Havana. You had to know where to look for the faded wooden plaque, nearly hidden by a drooping eave. EL ROSARIO—FABRICA DE TABACO, it proclaimed with tarnished pride.

Raul coaxed the truck's bald tires up onto the curb. Rounding the truck bed, he patted the rolled tent. "Smells good, eh, amigo?" he said out loud, drawing in the pungent aroma of aged tobacco escaping through holes and cracks in the skewed structure. He moved toward the building's large, wooden door, pushed it open, and stepped inside.

The mottled outward appearance of the building yielded within to soft, effective, overhead lighting. Twenty wooden worktables spanned the large room, facing the door. Each table was divided into four work stations occupied by men and women, their skin the color of Moroccan leather. The men wore stained sleeveless undershirts or loose-fitting, short-sleeved shirts that had once been white. The women were topped in faded prints that had once burst with color. Many of them smoked the results of their labor. In a relaxed, steady rhythm, they rolled the piles of brown leaves splayed in front of them into new cigars.

A dark pulpit imposed itself at the head of the room, just to Raul's right, inside the door. There, a heavy woman, *la lectora,* sat reading in a robust voice to the intent assembly. At the moment she was turning a page of an open newspaper. A pile of newspapers and magazines waited in front of her.

Raul closed the door behind him, and *la lectora*'s animated recital of baseball scores came to an abrupt halt. A soft clacking filled the room as the *torcedores* tapped their chavetas against the wooden tables.

"Señor Salazar!" the reader called, beaming. The *torcedores'* tapped greeting faded as many pairs of white or yellowed eyes reflected the lights above.

She stepped down from her stool, casting a stern look across the room. The *tabaqueros* regrasped their tools and the gentle work resumed.

"So soon?" she asked. "You just took fifteen boxes three weeks ago. Business must be good, very good!"

Since the embargo, there had been a brisk demand for the hand-rolled cigars crafted in the small factories of Little Havana, particularly those like El Rosario, which still drew from their warehouse of previously imported Cuban tobacco. Raul had seven boxes of his recent purchase of El Rosarios left. When his own stock of true Cubans was gone, which would be in a matter of days, he would easily sell fifteen boxes of the El Rosarios in much less than three weeks. But after that, when the Cuban tobacco in the sheds of Little Havana was gone, the boom would end.

"I wish that were so, Señora. No, this time I have come about something else. Is Señor Torres here?"

Her disappointment flickered briefly, then she stepped down and regally strolled the few steps to a door behind the podium. She knocked softly, nodded to Raul, and returned to her stool.

The door opened.

The old man's tan, weathered face was in sharp contrast with his white linen suit. His broad, silk tie flourished in brocaded splendor against a tailored, lime-colored shirt. Pleasure warmed Raul, and he clasped his grandfather's best friend in a firm embrace.

"Raul, my son. Welcome!" the old man said, in a voice softened by what Raul could only guess must be around eighty-five years.

"Ernesto, you are a tribute to all that is civilized," said Raul. He stood away and held onto the older one's forearms, admiring the perfection of stature and dress before him.

"Ah," Ernesto Torres demurred, "señoritas and cigars. They have been kind to me. That is true. But evening is finally here and soon my midnight will come, as it does for us all. Come, sit down."

The old man closed the door and moved to his desk, a rich mahogany table. Its gleaming surface was studded with neat piles of yellow paper slips bearing handwritten scrawls. Raul recognized them as the tags identifying fields of origin and harvest dates of tobacco bundles from the Vuelta Abajo, Cuba's inland tobacco treasure house. As a boy Raul had helped his grandfather print slips like these and attach them to bundles. It was said that Jennaro Salazar had originated this "system," such as it was.

"It is nice to see some things that do not change," Raul said, sweeping his hand over the desk.

"Yes, Raul. Your grandfather's way has served us well. Like labels on fine wine. But, sadly, it is ending." He laid his hand on a small pile about two inches high. "These represent the last *hoja de fortaleza* we have from Cuba, the last of our leaves of strength and flavor. I am afraid that the Norte Americanos will not change their policy toward Cuba for many, many years. Next week we start using tobacco from other countries. Nothing will ever be the same."

*So,* Raul thought, *even sooner than I had expected.* Yes, he had been right. His business could not help but strangle in the choke hold of the embargo. What good was a fine Cuban restaurant without fine Cuban cigars?

Belying the funereal tone of his soft voice, the old man's eyes sparkled from their dark crevices. Clearly, he was pleased at the visit from his old friend's grandson.

"What brings you to El Rosario so soon, Raul? Did you not just make a purchase from us?"

Raul nodded. "Yes, Ernesto. But today I am here to ask a favor. A very special favor. One that will bring the blessings of my father and grandfather down upon you. Someday, when we are all together, we will laugh over it."

Ernesto Torres made the sign of the cross and shook

his head sadly. "Ah, your grandfather, God rest his good soul. Jennaro taught me everything. If only he had listened to me! When the gangsters came, I told him it was only a matter of time. And look what happened. They murdered his son and stole his lands. He could have been here, working side by side with me all these years. Instead, he died alone and penniless, a trespasser in his own fields. When they took your father, their cruel knife cut out your grandfather's heart as well. Stripped of you both, he had nothing to live for."

Raul hesitated. Friends of Paulo had sent news of his grandfather's death a month after he'd landed in Miami. There had been no details.

"You know of Jennaro's death . . . how he died?"

Ernesto Torres embraced Raul with his eyes. "Yes, I know. We shared many friends, as you know." Reading the torment in Raul's expression, he continued.

"Within hours of murdering Victor, the gangster, Bonafaccio, was at Batista's side. He asked that all the Salazar properties be forfeited to him as payment for his services to Cuba and as compensation for Victor's thievery. The story goes that he and Batista enjoyed a good laugh over that and then Batista drafted a decree granting Jennaro's lands and the Salazar Fabrica to Bonafaccio.

"The next day the Mafia snake took his men and drove to San Luis. They found Jennaro at the warehouse and drove him out, laughing and beating him with sticks. Bonafaccio showed him the paper signed by Batista and told him the only way he would return to his fields would be as a laborer, working for Bonafaccio. It is said that Jennaro picked himself up from the dirt, laughed in Bonafaccio's face, and walked away. He was found a week later, dead, in the middle of one of his fields—a heart attack they said."

The old man's eyes glazed as he pictured what might have been. Then he looked directly at Raul. "Of course, I will do you any favor. Tell me what you need."

Raul sat down. "First, I must tell you a story," he said quietly, "of why my grandfather was able to laugh at Bonafaccio and of our dear friend Paulo. It will help if you know."

Raul left the El Rosario factory forty-five minutes later, lacking conviction that his fragile thread of a plan would withstand the coming strain. He wondered whether those surreal minutes after discovering Paulo had laid waste to his reason. Common sense told him to forget the Don Salazarios, as Rosa had begged. Bonafaccio's deadly net would soon close, and any sane man would flee for his life, satisfied with the money teased from Gessleman. Paulo's horrible sacrifice had made that option unthinkable.

Raul now knew that his sliver of a chance had opened when Joseph Bonafaccio and Dominick Romelli had disembarked at Kingston. Paulo's anesthetic must have been his knowledge that Raul would return that morning to Miami and that by directing his torturers to Kingston he was buying his employer precious time. The hunters would miss their prey—for now.

As Raul reached Paulo's truck, he again smoothed his hand across the tarped bundle in the pickup bed. He thought of the early morning quiet before a bullfight, bro-

ken only by the *encierro,* the delivery of the bulls from
the ranch where they were raised to the ring where they
would be fought. "Thank you, my friend," he said, "for
the *encierro.*" Paulo had delivered the Bonafaccio bull to
Raul. Now he must fight it.

Normally it took less than twenty minutes to reach Key
Biscayne—but that was in the Bonneville. Paulo's truck
protested whenever the needle behind the cracked speed-
ometer approached forty-five miles per hour. Rattles and
knocks signaling terminal engine failure passed through the
fire wall, while gears and shafts, long weary of meshing
with each other, whined through gaps in the oil-stained
floorboards. Raul fought his impatience as the familiar
miles ground by in maddening slow motion. He couldn't
help but contrast what he knew would be the speed of Bonafaccio's fury when he learned Raul had fled Kingston.
Each minute for Raul would be seconds for Bonafaccio.

He sighed with relief as the hour-long ordeal from Little
Havana wheezed to an end and he pulled into the marina
parking lot. After locating a dolly outside the harbormaster's office, he loaded the bulky tarp onto it. Satisfied the
load looked sufficiently nautical to appease any curious on-
looker, he wheeled down the ramp to the slip and slowly
pushed Paulo toward the *Don Salazario.*

The twenty-eight-foot fishing boat bobbed gently at its
mooring as an early afternoon breeze rattled riggings and
outriggers throughout the harbor. Raul unsnapped and
stowed the blue canvas that sloped from the rear of the
cabin. Then he stepped back onto the adjacent finger of
dock and carefully slid the bundle from the dolly to the
stern of the boat. After that, he entered the cabin.

Immediately, he knew that Paulo had succeeded. The sliding hasp to the compartment built under the bench seat was pointing down. It was a quirk of Raul's to turn it up when securing it.

Quickly, he unlatched the compartment. He lifted the seat, and his breath caught at the sight. There, nestled in the seat nook, were three richly decorated boxes of Don Salazarios—the cigars Cornelius Gesselman had traded for the gilded Sancho Panzas.

"Thank you, Paulo, thank you," he whispered, thinking of those terrible last minutes when Paulo must have known he could have bought the sweet death of a bullet in exchange for the cigars.

There was no need to open the boxes. He knew his father's treasure was there. Besides, he had no intention of sacrificing any more of them to the frenzied discovery of the night before. Each one would be lovingly smoked for its prize.

Raul went astern and began to drag the cumbersome bundle into the cabin. After stowing Paulo's tent-shrouded body in the narrow passage, Raul took the cigars, locked the cabin door, and stepped onto the dock. He did not refasten the canvas cover. He raised his hand in salute toward the cabin.

"When I return," he said, "to send you to your final rest, my friend, I will be in a hurry. Until then, adios."

Raul looked around and confirmed that he had not been observed. Carrying the three boxes back to the pickup, he steeled himself for the return drive to Miami. This time he would not be in such a hurry. And he had yet another stop to make.

# TWENTY-FIVE

IT HAD TAKEN Cornelius Gessleman two hours to commandeer an airplane and a pilot brash enough to challenge the winter storm.

Enduring the turbulent passage south with gritted teeth and a death-claw grip on each armrest, every violent soar and plunge that buffeted the twin-engine Cessna further widened the vents of his anger. He drew comfort only from the anticipated news that his bumbling son-in-law no longer drew breath.

Gessleman snorted aloud, recalling how he had shoved the miserable bootlicker aside on the Hyannis tarmac. "What about me?" Wesley had croaked. "Get your own plane, asshole," he'd retorted, the satisfaction of leaving his son-in-law standing there shivering a mere fraction of the pleasure he would feel when Dominick Romelli called to confirm his Wesley's untimely demise.

Now, straining in his seat, grimacing at every surge,

dhe began to realize that Wesley's death would not be enough. The whole cigar fiasco had simply exacerbated his impatience with Wesley's bumbling. If it had not been the cigars, it would have been something else. Wesley was like that: doomed to succeed at failure.

What emerged as the *real* source of his displeasure was that he had forked over one hundred thousand dollars to that assassin-blackmailer Raul Salazar for the Kennedy cigars, which were now in the clutches of some hick sheriff.

Suddenly, Gessleman stiffened, this time not from the turbulence. How had that sheriff managed to appear on the scene precisely as Salazar's "amigos" were delivering the cigars to Gessleman? Of course! It had been a setup from the outset! Salazar had shrewdly let the cigars remain in Massachusetts because he was in cahoots with the sheriff. How else could the Cuban's so-called "professionals" have pulled off a burglary of the Kennedy estate?

His face mirroring the darkening hues outside the aircraft's cabin, Gessleman pondered this for several minutes. Then a narrow smile split his grim features. The answer didn't matter. He was not quite done redeeming favors from the Bonafaccios.

He recalled young Joseph's passion for fine cigars. The iron reputation of Joe Senior had been forged from the retribution visited ruthlessly on those who had cheated him. Certainly Joseph Junior would be sympathetic to the plight of an old man who had been in his father's favor, an old man cheated by the son of the man who had cheated the Bonafaccios. It was little more to ask that

Bonafaccio extract a refund of Gessleman's one hundred thousand from Salazar before handing the slick Cuban blackmailer his last cigar.

Finally, as the beautiful symmetry of it all settled in, Cornelius Gessleman began to chuckle. How fitting that he not only would recover his losses but would also bring down the president's assassin! He would see that history received a polished version of his role so future generations could pay grateful homage to his memory.

His chuckling swelled to a hacking crescendo. Old Don Bonafaccio had been a conspicuous patriot and close friend of Joseph Kennedy. The Bonafaccios would no doubt deal with Raul Salazar in their own painfully special way before letting him die. Cornelius might just present young Joseph with a gift: one of the boxes of Sancho Panzas. Then again, maybe he wouldn't.

As the beleaguered aircraft drove though waves of sleet and skirted mountainous thunderheads, the struggling pilot was momentarily distracted by a noise behind him. He glanced quickly over his shoulder and, at first, thought he was witnessing the fear of God striking a skinny old man panicked by the raging storm. Then, amazed, he realized his passenger was convulsed in hysterical laughter as Gessleman's explosive peals greeted each fresh flash of lightning.

# TWENTY-SIX

"FINGERS, WE'RE NOT leaving until we find that thieving sonofabitch and get those diamonds." Joseph Bonafaccio Jr. folded his hands across his chest as they threaded their way through Miami's afternoon traffic toward Little Havana and Noches Cubanas.

During the long course of Dominick Romelli's service to the Bonafaccio's, he had been called upon to handle just about everything friends and enemies of the Bonafaccio family could conceivably devise. With the unfolding transition from Mafia bosses to entrepreneuring capitalists, Dominick had been pleased to see most of the old ways fall away—the feral violence gradually replaced by the reasoned, bloodless power of money. The old ways led to prison; the new style led to flattering pieces in the *Wall Street Journal*.

Romelli's young employer had always been the epitome of the new leadership, his Columbia pedigree and instinctive ease in the loftiest towers of finance cutting him off from the paths of the past. Until now.

A powerful sense of déjà vu overcame Romelli. For an instant, it was the Don seated next to him, not the educated, urbane son who had been so carefully groomed to inherit the Bonafaccio empire.

As traffic permitted, Romelli continued his clandestine study of Joseph Jr.'s face, noting the eyes were narrowed in a countenance of anger and revenge. Joseph seemed possessed by his untapped heritage—the code of the Sicilian hills that refused to accept honorable defeat, where retribution had been spit with a fiery, two-barreled blast from a Lupo. Romelli knew he would be unable to dissuade Joseph from his quest, but hoped he might yet protect him from it.

"Joseph, when we catch up with Salazar, maybe I should do the talking. You're too involved, too emotional about this. Hell, you're *wearing* the guy!" Joseph shot him a black look. Romelli continued.

"Remember, it's only business. It was his *father* who stole from the Family, not him. We've got no reason to hurt Salazar.

"Of course, it's complicated by this Gessleman's petition that I kill him. But again, that's strictly business. What do we gain by carrying out this contract? Obviously, I can't kill Salazar until he turns over the diamonds and his family's debt is paid. Then our only reason to kill him would be your father's pledge to Gessleman. Is that enough? What would your father want? Remember, the Don cared for Victor Salazar and was saddened to learn of his treachery. He decided the kid shouldn't pay for his father's crime. Would he want us to kill him now? When we used to take on contracts we always screened them for conflicts of interest. Seems to me we've got sort of a conflict here."

Traffic stopped and Romelli stole another glance at Joseph. He could see that his words were falling on deaf ears. When Joseph spoke, his voice was from another time.

"Fingers, are you going soft on me? Come on! This guy's father screwed us out of three million dollars! And Salazar knows where it's at! Why else would old 'Mr. P' fight so hard last night to keep Salazar's whereabouts a secret? Why the cat-and-mouse chase from Jamaica? We put up with bullshit like this and we stand to lose a helluva lot more than the lousy three million. This guy's as dirty as his father, and he's gonna get the same treatment. Just as soon as we get the diamonds. I mean it. We cut whatever deal he wants. Sure, why not? But once we get those diamond cigars, all bets are off. He dies. And we collect Gessleman's hundred grand to boot."

Dominick Romelli nodded patiently. Nothing was going to shake Joseph from his course. It wouldn't do any good to tell him that Raul Salazar was far too smart to surface at Noches Cubanas. Let the kid spend a few long, sticky days staking out the joint. Joseph thinks the old days were all action and muscle. He'll learn. Most of it was long sessions in stuffy cars, especially with a wily target like Salazar.

*What the hell*, he thought. *Maybe the kid has a point.*

I am *getting soft*. No one *cheats the Bonafaccios. Joseph is, after all, his father's son. When it came to "business," the Don had always been right. Always.*

Romelli focused on the crawling traffic and began to plan the two jobs to come. No messy stuff this time. Just nice, clean, long-range hits. It had been his favorite work.

Raul stopped the gasping truck at a scrolled iron gate with a flowing capital N crafted into the bars. Out of curiosity, he had first located the home of his father's old friend several years earlier. There had been no reason to disturb the old man's seclusion—until now.

There was no address. Few Palm Beach residences displayed one.

Raul pulled close to the speaker box mounted on an adobe column and pressed the button. After ten seconds a young woman's voice answered, her voice creamy and mellowed by a Spanish accent. "Yes? Who is it?"

Raul leaned from the truck window toward the speaker. "Señorita, my name is Raul Salazar. My father was a friend of Señor Nuñez. I need to speak with him. It is very important."

There was a pause. Then, "Señor Nuñez says he has never heard of you. You must have the wrong person. I am sorry."

Raul opened the driver's door and stood, his mouth almost touching the speaker. It was important that he be precisely understood. There was no time to come at this ghost of the past from another direction. He was positive he had puzzled out the key to Victor Salazar's belated triumph over the Bonafaccios: Felipe Nuñez.

"Señorita, wait. Please. Tell Señor Nuñez that my father was Victor Salazar. Tell him we met one night long ago, in Havana, at Noches Cubanas, when I was introduced to my father's friend, Javier Menendez."

The speaker was silent for half a minute. Then, without announcement, the ponderous gate swung open. Raul climbed back in the truck and drove toward the four-story adobe hacienda, bracketed in the foreground by stately palms. Beyond spilled the glare of sand.

As he approached the shaded, brick entry, a set of large French doors on one side opened and an olive-skinned woman in her late thirties appeared, guiding a wheelchair. In the chair, a shawl covering his legs, sat a frail, much older man.

The woman wheeled the man onto the veranda that spanned the front of the building. She was dressed in loose, white slacks and a matching blouse.

Driving closer, Raul feared he may have been wrong. The emaciated husk before him bore little resemblance to the man he remembered from long ago.

Raul switched off the ignition and sighed at the truck motor's death rattle as it expired on its own terms.

The old man clapped twice, his hoarse laugh nearly lost in the light breeze. "What a wonderful sound! I had one just like it many years ago. It, too, always spoke to me after I told it to stop."

Raul climbed out and mounted the steps. The woman studied him with an intense curiosity. The man reached up and patted her hand on the chair handle. "It is all right, Maria," he said. "I recognize him. It is Victor's son." Then, extending his hand, he said, "You are either a remarkable detective or your father shared with you our secret, a secret known only to one other living person." He looked up at the woman, who returned his smile.

The sharp eyes and long, delicate fingers of the man he had met fifteen years earlier were now apparent to Raul. His father had remarked then that the man's eyes and hands were the tools of his treasured craft. Raul wondered whether they'd survived whatever had ravaged the rest of him.

"Yes, Señor Nuñez, my father told me about you, but not everything. Only in the last twenty-four hours have the pieces come together, and I now know why he never told me more. It would have endangered both of us."

The old man regarded Raul thoughtfully. Then, nodding his head toward the study behind them, he said, "Come. Strong reasons must have brought you here. They are best discussed inside, over a glass of sherry."

Maria turned the wheelchair and Raul followed them through the French doors into the book-lined study. After filling two crystal glasses, she handed one to Nuñez and one to Raul. She took a seat next to the wheelchair, while Raul sat across from the two of them. He raised his glass.

"To your health, Señor Felipe Nuñez Javier Menendez."

The old man lifted his glass and smiled. "Shhh, we do not use that name here. Thanks to your father, I was able to leave Javier Menendez behind, long ago, in the Caribbean."

Nuñez sipped from the glass and set it down. Then his sharp eyes narrowed and he fixed on Raul a gaze that penetrated to Raul's soul. "I hope you are not here to resurrect him."

Hastening to put his host at ease, Raul shook his head emphatically. "No, no. Nothing like that. Your secret is safer now than it ever has been. I have no reason to expose you. In fact, keeping your secret is critical to my own plans. As you will see."

Raul drained the rest of his sherry.

"No," he continued, "What I need now are your skills. The saga of the diamonds you cut and sold my father continues. It was supposed to have played out long ago, when my father thought he could get them out of Cuba."

Nuñez leaned forward, nodding, concentrating. His intensity was that of a child enraptured by a good story. Raul continued, noting Maria was also hanging on his every word. Apparently sensing her concern, Nuñez reached up and covered her hand.

"After my father bought the diamonds from you, he had my grandfather roll them inside some of his cigars. My father must have intended to send them to me after he was sure I was safe in Miami."

Raul paused. Through the open doors, a freshening breeze rustled the slender palms encircling the veranda.

"My call was never answered. He miscalculated the impatience of the Bonafaccios. They murdered him within hours of sending me from Cuba. The cigars with the diamonds stayed in my father's humidor room. The Bonafaccios looted it when Castro drove them out."

Again, Raul paused, his mouth dry from the telling of

what he had pieced together. Maria filled his glass. He softened his tongue and continued.

"Incredibly, the cigars with the diamonds have now surfaced. Fate, luck, maybe even a curse, have brought them to me, as my father intended. The Americanos and their embargo have forced Castro further into the embrace of the Russians and have caused serious deprivations that will kill many of our innocent countrymen. Children die every day for want of medicine and food. These diamonds can make a difference, and I am determined they will do so. But I will need your help."

Maria's eyes filled. Nuñez stroked her hand and spoke.

"We know well what you say. I met Maria at Santiago's carnival in 1954, the same year I met your father. I had just come to Cuba and was still living the life of a phantom, fleeing the long tentacles of Winston's and the U.S. authorities. I had a fortune in uncut diamonds, but no way to sell them.

"As my friendship with your father grew, we shared confidences. When the Bonafaccios forced their way into his business, he knew it would only be a matter of time before they took everything. He began to divert money, a little at first, then, when he thought he had perfected a channel, large sums. As he did this, he paid me for the diamonds I cut for him. He helped me establish a new identity and a new life."

The old man raised his hand in a sweeping gesture, including Maria. "Your father made all of this possible.

"Maria has two sisters. Both have lost their infant children to disease because of Cuba's shortages. We tried to send money, but it never reached them. If you think you can help others, then God be with you."

Raul nodded. "Yes, I have a way," he said. "Like you, I will have a new life. Let me tell you what I need. First, please examine these and tell me what you see."

Raul removed a knotted white linen handkerchief from his shirt pocket and handed it to Nuñez. The old man motioned with his head to Maria. She wheeled him over to a small table in the corner of the study. Raul followed and watched slender brown fingers with alabaster pads carefully pick the wadded cloth apart. The four stones Raul had discovered tumbled in a gentle glissade onto a black velvet cloth.

The old jeweler hunched over them for several seconds, turning one, then another, before the magnifyied inquisition of his loupe. Then he sat upright, a sad smile spreading across his tanned face.

"Yes, Raul, these are four of one hundred diamonds I sold your father. I cut these diamonds myself, of that I am positive. If you have the rest of them, you possess a fortune. Is that all you require of me?"

"No, Señor," Raul whispered. Drawing a breath, he exhaled slowly. "There is more."

# TWENTY-SEVEN

DAWN PENETRATED THE storm-troubled sky, bestowing a rose-and-crimson blush. As Raul drove from the darkened hacienda, he wondered if Rosa was watching the same spectacle. He savored the day's beginning, knowing it might well be his last.

Many times during the long night the old man had faltered and nodded in exhaustion. Maria had seen him through—always at his side, her voice prodding in quiet encouragement. Raul hoped he was now getting the rest he had so richly earned. As for Raul, sleep would have to wait. There was still much to do.

At 4:30 A.M. there was no traffic, and the drive south rimming three counties passed quickly, even in Paulo's truck. Raul made the Miami city limits at 5:45 and drove directly to Little Havana, staying on back streets and away from the neighborhood of Noches Cubanas. He was not yet ready to confront Joseph Bonafaccio. That would come soon enough. When they met, it would not be in the early dawn at an empty restaurant.

El Rosario was just awakening, the *tabaqueros* drifting in by twos and threes, plumed curls from the day's first smoke drifting behind them. *Here, nothing has changed,* thought Raul, remembering his grandfather's workers and their unlimited access to the finest product of their labors.

Ernesto Torres was at one of the work stations, his back erect in the forced posture of one who has spent many hours seated. The sleeves of his fine shirt were rolled above his elbows, and a gray stubble spoke of his night-long toil. He looked up as Raul approached the bench.

"So, were you successful?" Ernesto's voice was a whisper against the salutations of the *tabaqueros* filing into the long room, tarrying before beginning their work.

"Yes," said Raul, setting before the old cigar maker the three boxes of Don Salazarios recently retrieved from the boat.

"You can see that one box has been opened and four cigars are missing. Everything else is intact, just as my grandfather made them."

"Good," said Ernesto. "And the rest?"

Raul drew a cloth bag from his pocket and set it on top of one of the boxes.

"Excellent!" beamed the old man. "I have also been busy." He gestured toward several neatly stacked piles of tobacco leaves filling the stations on each side of him.

"Now you should get some rest. It will be many hours

before I am done. Go. Use the couch in my office. I will come for you when all is ready."

Raul laid a hand on the old man's shoulder. Their eyes met in tacit understanding. Raul should sleep while Ernesto awakened ebbed skills to save his life.

"He'll come back here, Dominick, he has to. He's just staying away to make us believe he's been here and gone. This crafty spic's just like his father, too smart for his own good. The diamonds are still here somewhere. I can smell 'em."

The two of them sat in the rented car, a half block down the street from Noches Cubanas. Bonafaccio pulled a cigar case from his pocket, slid it open, and offered one to Romelli.

"No thanks, Joseph. Too early for me. Tell you what, though. I'm going to take a walk to that coffee shop up the street and get a couple of donuts or something. Coffee?"

"Yeah, that'd be great. Thanks, Dom. Keep an eye down here, though, in case he shows up."

Romelli nodded. "Will do." He got out of the car.

"Oh, hey, Dominick," Joseph said through the open window, looking at his watch. It was a few minutes before 9:00 A.M. "Lisa should be in the office by now, probably be a good idea if you called her, just to check in.

Romelli returned to the car fifteen minutes later with two cups of coffee and a bag of apple fritters. He slid into the front seat, smiling.

"You're not going to believe this," he said, passing one of the cups to Joseph.

"Gessleman called first thing this morning from Kentucky. Lisa said he was all hot and bothered about something, so I returned his call. Says he wants to talk to us before I do the jobs on his son-in-law and Salazar. I told him we were in Miami, and he assumed we were here for the hits. He got excited and told me to hold off until he talks to us, in person. Says he still wants the jobs done but needs something *extra*. Wouldn't go into it on the phone. I told him I'd call him later to arrange a meeting."

Romelli stuffed half a fritter in his mouth and washed it down with a gulp of coffee. "Oh," he added. "I told him 'extras' cost extra and to get at least three hundred grand together as advance payment. We'll collect it when we meet."

Bonafaccio grinned and patted his mentor-employee on the shoulder. "Fingers, you're something else," he said. "Always thinking."

Raul looked up into the core of hot sun searing the dusty floor of the Plaza de Toros. Momentarily blinded, he glanced toward his feet, planted in the red soil. The bullfighter's delicate, slipperlike shoes came into focus. They seemed ridiculously suited for engaging the enraged animal, in whose eyes of red hate he now saw his reflection. The *traje de luces* shone in the bull's eyes, its shimmering sequins catching the bright sun and inflaming the beast even more.

A ragged drool of red-tinged gore hung from the side of the bull's open mouth and its thick tongue probed to cleanse this further annoyance before returning to the afternoon's deadly work.

Raul's eyes cleared as he slowly maneuvered between the bull and the sun. He focused on the massive head, his eyes fixed to the bull's. Something else, though, fought for his attention. There, from behind the bull, rolling toward him in the dirt, two bloody objects, coming closer.

The first one stopped at his feet. He knelt and his fingers closed on thick strands. He lifted and the tendrils tightened with the awful weight they bore. His father's face stared back at him, peaceful and reassuring, though jagged ribbons of flesh and blood streaked the neck.

The second object rolled to stillness, and again he reached into the hot dirt at his feet. This time he pulled up Paulo's head. Paulo's lips were compressed in a tight, resigned smile, his dark, eyeless sockets staring vacantly.

Then Raul heard a song. Not the brassy celebration of the bullring, but the lilting soprano of children. At the tip of his vision, in the seats above the ring, he saw a cluster of children surrounding a woman: Rosa. Their song was hauntingly familiar.

Suddenly, the bull was upon him, immense and grinning. Raul felt himself swept up, riding the great horns into the sun, their points tearing his flesh as they carried him higher. Then the bull twisted its head and slammed him to the dirt, the horns ripping, goring, shaking, shaking . . .

"Raul! Raul!" Ernesto Torres lightly shook Raul once again by the shoulder. "I am done. Wake up and look."

Raul left Little Havana, again staying well clear of Noches Cubanas. The restaurant staff would be showing up soon, wondering why neither he nor Paulo was there to orchestrate their nightly ritual. Mindful that Bonafaccio was probably waiting, he had not called.

*They will know what to do,* he told himself. *Henry, the dishwasher, will tend bar, as we have taught him to do in a pinch. Rafael will cook, as usual. Perhaps he will do a limited menu. Rafael's assistant, Cruz, will be the host.*

This time, because of the Friday afternoon traffic, the drive to Key Biscayne did not seem so onerous. Paulo's truck crept along with the best of them, a steady stream of automobiles emptying the city for the weekend.

Restored by the fitful sleep at El Rosario, Raul used the time to once again ponder the events of the past week and where they were taking him. It was difficult to shake the haunting images of his dream.

On a long-ago, hot summer morning in the Vuelta Abajo, minutes before Victor Salazar and eight-year-old Raul left for Raul's first bullfight, Lucia Salazar had knelt next to her son, her soft voice filled with a mother's wisdom.

"Remember, son, the bull was created by God, too. It has a heart and a soul like you. It is right to feel sad for the bull when it is over."

After that day, in the rough corral that served as the town's Plaza de Toros, Raul grew to love the ceremony and pathos of the bullfight. His fondest memories of his father were of their many *temporadas.* Together they had pursued the bullfighting seasons to Mexico City and, later, to Spain. Victor's success with Noches Cubanas made it possible for the two aficionados to enjoy their shared passion on a grand scale. Madrid, Seville, Ronda, and Bilbao became an annual pilgrimage. His mother's advice, given before that first *corrida,* stayed with Raul throughout these journeys. He respected the bull, always.

Fragments of the dream at El Rosario continued to invade Raul's thoughts as he neared Key Biscayne. *Madre de Dios*, what a dance this was!

He stopped at the pay phone by the marina entrance and checked his watch: 6:15. Pedro and Jorgé should be back from Cape Cod by now. Nothing could keep Jorgé from the weekend races at Hialeah, especially with ten thousand dollars of Gessleman's money burning a hole in his pocket. Raul dialed the number of La Paloma.

The bartender shouted over the animated din of La Paloma's mariachi guitars and trumpets celebrating the week's end.

"*SÍ! BUENAS TARDES!* LA PALOMA."

"Gregorio, this is Raul. Are Pedro and Jorgé back?"

"Ah, Raul. *Sí.* Jorgé is back. He is right here. Wait."

In a few seconds, Jorgé was on the line.

"Raul! How is Jamaica? You should be making love at this time of day, not calling your friends. But I am glad you did. I stopped by the restaurant and no one knows where Paulo is. His truck is gone. Did he go fishing?"

Raul responded tersely, his voice a sharp contrast to the celebration on the other end.

"Jorgé, I cannot tell you right now what has happened. I will meet you at La Paloma in one hour and give you something to take to Noches Cubanas. I want you to take four or five hombres, big ones, with you. Get them together now, and I will see you at La Paloma in one hour and explain. Understood?"

"*Sí,* Raul. Here, in one hour. There are plenty of hombres here already. I will pick out the best."

"Is Pedro with you?" Raul asked.

Jorgé laughed. "No, Pedro stayed up north. He is in love. The señorita from Cape Cod. Ah, Raul, we had such an adventure! You would not believe it. The sheriff swooped down on us like a cormorant, just as we were giving the cigars to Señor Gessleman."

Raul shook his head. He had no time for this.

Obviously his delegates had not been arrested if one of them was making love and the other was spending his usual Friday night tossing back Cuba libres. The story could wait.

"Okay, Jorgé, tell me later. I will see you there in an hour. Adios."

Dominick Romelli polished off his third *taco de carnitas,* tilted the seat back as far as it would go, and slid his hat down over his eyes. By 6:00 P.M. he was convinced Raul Salazar had reunited somewhere in the Caribbean with his señorita and that the Bonafaccio cigar diamonds were history. It had all seemed a fairy tale to him anyway.

The only real loss, he thought, was the fee from Gessleman for doing Salazar. Or *was* it lost? If Salazar *was* gone, he *could* just tell Gessleman he had carried out the job. How would Gessleman know the difference? Sure, make up some gruesome story and . . . Naa, good way to destroy a reputation.

He watched the entrance to Noches Cubanas as five boisterous Castro haters entered the restaurant. *God, Manhattan is going to look good,* he thought.

"You got it, Boss? I'm going to catch a little shut-eye."
*Hell, it was the kid's show. He didn't need Romelli's eyes,
only his gun, and that appeared unlikely now.*

"Yeah, Dom. Go ahead. I'll wake you when he shows.
Shouldn't be long."

*Right,* thought Romelli, conjuring up the image of that
shapely little Lisa back in Joseph's Manhattan office. *You'll
learn, kid. Guy as slick as this Salazar isn't going to be
hanging around with the Bonafaccio family breathing
down his neck. Don't think so.*

In what seemed like thirty seconds, but what his watch
told him was an hour, Romelli felt Joseph's hand on his
arm.

"Dom! He's here. I'm sure that's him—driving that
wreck of a truck parked in the alley last night."

Romelli blinked his eyes open. He watched the truck
climb the curb and the lights flicker off. Raul Salazar
stepped out and looked around.

"I'll be damned," Romelli said, suddenly bristling with
energy, proud of his boss's tenacity. He would be able to
score the hit for Gessleman after all. Then it struck him:
There was still a financial wrinkle to iron out.

It had been Romelli's practice to keep the entire fee
for jobs he performed as an independent contractor. Here,
where his services were sought in satisfaction of a long-
ago pledge by the Don, he was in a gray area. In a sense,
it was Family business, and then again, it wasn't. De-
pended on how you looked at it.

Dominick Romelli was a true professional. With this
kind of work, everyone involved had to have a clear understanding of the terms and conditions in advance. Ter-

minal results were irreversible. Suddenly Romelli was relieved by Gessleman's postponement. It would give him time to discuss the fee arrangement with Joseph.

Another advantage of the delay was that Romelli would not be forced to drop Salazar in his own restaurant. Hits on the target's home turf were to be avoided. Romelli was convinced his strict adherence to this rule had contributed to his long and healthy life.

The prospect of taking Salazar for one of those famous New York "rides" similarly held little appeal. Romelli much preferred that he watch Gessleman's son-in-law and Salazar meet their ends through the fine precision of a Bausch & Lomb scope.

"We'll give him a couple of minutes after he goes in, Joseph. Always better to let the mouse think he's made it safely back to the hole. If we're lucky, he'll go right for the cheese we couldn't find last night."

It gratified Dominick Romelli to pass this bit of street wisdom along to Joseph, who was always quick to tell him how to invest his money.

# TWENTY-EIGHT

RAUL CHECKED HIS watch as he entered Noches Cubanas: 9:10. Cruz was on duty as maître d'; and Jorgé, together with four large friends, had revived the celebration Raul had interrupted when he'd met them an hour earlier at La Paloma. Drinks and cigars flashed as well-worn arguments and jokes were dusted off and enjoyed again.

Jorgé nodded to Raul, who winked back as he passed through the arched opening.

"Señor Raul!" Cruz exclaimed. "You're back from your trip already? And Paulo? He is not with you?"

"No, of course not. You mean he is not here?"

The assistant-chef-turned-maître d' shrugged his shoulders, his palms upward. "No one knows where he is. When we closed last night, he was here with four men I did not know. Bad hombres. He said everything was all right and that he would lock up. He did not show up for work today. It is very strange."

"Yes," said Raul. "That is not like him at all. You have called him?"

"*Sí*, many times. There is no answer."

Satisfied with his charade, Raul turned and climbed the stairs leading to his office. Halfway up he paused, turned, and came back down. He went into the kitchen and approached Rafael, who was working at the stove.

Raul placed a hand on his chef's shoulder. "Rafael, *uno momento por favor.*" Rafael grinned and stepped away from the stove.

Five minutes later, Raul left the kitchen and again started up to his office. This time he stopped at the head of the stairs, as the melodic herald of a lone trumpet rose from the jukebox in the bar: the announcement of the *toreros* entrance. He turned and looked down. Jorgé and his "four hombres" were looking up at him, and Rafael was poised at the kitchen door, smiling. His *cuadrilla* assembled, he was ready to face the bull. He had not missed the large sedan parked a block and a half away.

Dominick Romelli interlaced his fingers and pushed, popping his knuckles in rippling succession. "Okay, Joseph, time's up. Let's pay Mr. Salazar a visit and see about those diamond cigars you're so worked up about."

Bonafaccio started the engine and inched the car down the block. A car pulled from the curb and he took its place, parking almost in front of Noches Cubanas.

They stepped from the car and were instantly surrounded by the rich aroma of fine cigars. *By, God,* Joseph thought, *I haven't smelled anything like this since we left*

*Cuba.* There was nothing in New York to compare with the fragrance spilling from Noches Cubanas.

*"Buenas noches, Señores!"* boomed the maître d' as they entered.

The enthusiastic greeting drew a smile from Joseph in spite of himself. The restaurant had an incomparable character, and the perfume of strong cigars was unbelievable. This was not at all what had met them the night before, when empty tables and the gruesome business downstairs had blanketed the raucous charm of the place. *Too bad we're here on business again,* he thought. This was a spot he could enjoy. There sure as hell was nothing like it in Manhattan.

Romelli led off, his low voice leaving no room for negotiation. "Take us to Señor Salazar, now. No announcement. No bullshit." The maître d' smiled, in spite of Romelli's uncompromising menace.

"Of course, Señor. Follow me, please."

Joseph glanced at Dominick, who nodded. Romelli's eyes swept the interior as the maître d' led them upstairs to Raul's office. Joseph noted Romelli's deft assessment of their potential opposition; the handful of expatriates in the bar debating racing odds and baseball statistics were certainly no threat. He watched their lively gestures stir clouds of cigar smoke, exciting small tornadoes.

Halfway up the stairs, Joseph whispered to Romelli, his head inclining toward the passage leading down to the wine cellar. "Dom, do you think that guy's still down there?"

Romelli stopped, gave Joseph a long look, and shook his head. Joseph understood. Once a message like last night's was delivered, the recipient didn't keep the letter around; something else they had never taught him at Columbia.

Raul stiffened when he heard the footsteps on the stairs. It was suddenly a magnificent day in the summer of 1950, when Victor and Raul, then twenty-five, had followed the *temporada* to Bilbao. As he rose from his desk, the echo of phantom trumpets from that hot Plaza de Toros charged him with a brassy courage and determination.

It was fitting he should greet these murderers on his feet. His father's sage advice still held true: Respect was everything for these men. What was in your heart must remain hidden. If he adopted their charade of respect and honor, he might gain an edge in the precarious moments ahead.

Bonafaccio and Romelli stood in the doorway for several seconds as Raul faced them from behind his desk. "Thank you, Cruz," he finally said. "Set up for the three of us in the private room, will you?" Cruz's questioning eyes lingered on Raul, who nodded, sending him on his way.

Romelli spread his stocky bulk in front of the closed office door while Joseph crossed to Raul's desk and stepped behind it, edging Raul to one side. He commandeered Raul's chair and sat down, his feet propped comfortably on the desk. Toying with a dagger-shaped letter opener, he looked up.

"Yeah, Salazar. That'd be real nice. A couple of good cigars and a good dinner. Sort of celebrate our little reunion. But first you turn over what your old man stole from us, plus interest. Either five million dollars cash or the other three boxes of cigars with diamonds. Your choice."

Raul folded his arms and stood still, letting several silent seconds pass. The deadly dance had begun.

"What makes you think I have the money or these cigars you speak of? As you see, I run a simple business."

"Come on, Salazar, cut the crap. Too many arrows point straight to you. That little side step you gave us in Jamaica clinched it." Bonafaccio pointed the letter opener directly at Raul. "Your father's game is up. I want what he stole from us—now. After that, all is forgiven."

"Oh, really?" Raul asked. "Like with Paulo? He had neither money nor diamonds. I buried the pieces of your butchery this morning. Is that your forgiveness?"

Bonafaccio shrugged.

"Or suppose I *did* have these cigars you seek and I gave them to you—what then? Again, the same as Paulo, only perhaps without the torture? Don't both roads lead to the same place—a grave?"

Bonafaccio rolled his neck as if relieving a kink.

"You must know," Raul continued, "that I understand how your Family does business. You must think I am either very brave or very stupid to return here after what you did to poor Paulo. Well, I am neither."

Before pressing further, there was something Raul had to know. There was yet a piece missing, a very important piece. It might lie in the question he had put to Bonafaccio, still unanswered. He looked over at Romelli.

"May I sit down?" he asked.

Romelli left the door and crossed to Raul. He frisked him then nodded toward the chair in front of the desk. Raul sat, fixing Bonafaccio with an intent gaze.

"What makes you think I have either your money or diamonds?" he asked. "Many things could have brought me home from Jamaica."

Raul read nothing in the poker expression Bonafaccio offered. Then Joseph gave a what-the-hell shrug.

"Damnedest thing," he said. Then he lowered his feet to the floor and leaned forward. "Here we were, Dom and I, smoking a couple of those Don Salazario cigars your grandfather made. All of a sudden, a diamond plunks into the ashtray. Well . . ." His voice tightened and his expression softened.

"After Kennedy was killed"—again Bonafaccio's voice caught—"I had been thinking back to those days in Havana when we were in business with your father—you know, when the senator . . ."

Raul watched in disbelief as Bonafaccio's eyes clouded and he choked with emotion. In the several seconds that had passed since Bonafaccio had mentioned the slain president, a chameleon-like transformation had reduced the Mafia heir to near sobs. Raul had been prepared to confront a murderous gangster, not a mourning patriot. He stiffened, alert to some kind of ploy.

". . . When Senator Kennedy and those rat-pack friends of his used to come down and enjoy themselves," Bonafaccio finished, composing himself.

"So there I was, remembering better days with my father, Kennedy, all those people."

Bonafaccio stopped, his face again hardening.

"I had also been thinking of *your* father. Then I saw that diamond.

"So when Dom and I tore up the rest of the cigars and ended up with a pile of twenty-five diamonds, it was pretty clear how your old man had planned to get the money out of Cuba. Only he didn't. He had his 'accident,' and the cigars sat there in the big humidor room until Castro kicked Batista's butt and my family got the hell out.

"Of course we took all the cigars with us, and those few boxes of your grandfather's just got mixed in with the rest."

Raul shook his head, saddened by the image of the two Italians reducing a box of Don Salazario Presidentes to a pile of tan confetti.

Bonafaccio continued. "When Jack Kennedy visited us in Havana, he really enjoyed your grandfather's cigars. Then this past July, when he put out the word he wanted to stock up on good Cuban cigars, I gave him some, including the remaining three boxes of Don Salazarios. I'm pretty sure you've ended up with them. I don't know exactly how they came to you, but I'm not leaving here without them. Either that or . . ." He shrugged, the implication clear.

Raul frowned. This was the missing piece.

"Do you mind telling me *why* you think I have them?"

Bonafaccio sat back, relaxing, his mouth breaking into a broad smile. "Not at all! Seems you're a popular guy, only in the wrong way. Not long after we found the diamonds, Dominick got a call from an old business associate of the Don's. Seems he wants you dead. That did it for me. Another arrow pointed in your direction. First, the diamonds in your grandfather's cigars; then this guy Gessleman puts out a contract on you . . ."

Shock pulsed through Raul. Gessleman! *Madre de Dios!* How he had underestimated him. Then the chilling realization of *why* Bonafaccio was telling him this struck him. Bonafaccio was talking to a dead man. But first, he intended to extract his money or his diamonds.

"I take it you know the guy?" Bonafaccio asked.

Raul nodded, rapidly filling in the blanks. He realized he had just been handed an extra sword. He would need it. This bull was a killer, a *miura*, bred for deadly ferocity.

"So tell me, Salazar," Bonafaccio was asking, "how *did* you come to wind up with some of the cigars I gave the president, particularly cigars stuffed with diamonds?"

"Pardon?" replied Raul, the kaleidoscope still tumbling.

And then it formed, suddenly, beautifully.

Once again, he was in the arena, the matador resplendent in his *traje de luces*. The sequins flashed their challenge as the *toril* gates opened and the bull's muscular hulk stamped defiantly into the arena, dust rising from his gouging hooves.

"The diamonds, Salazar. How did you get them?"

Raul's focus sharpened with the bull's impatience. He knew what he must do: the mariposa, that tantalizing spell cast over the bull when the matador spreads his cape and glides backward, letting the cape's edges flow to the left and right of his exposed body like butterfly wings.

For the next fifteen minutes, Raul Salazar spun an intriguing story for Joseph Bonafaccio and Dominick Romelli. He told them of a Florida congressman and his wealthy father-in-law, two political fanatics whose hatred for Kennedy and envy of his private hoard of forbidden Cuban cigars had bred a contract of assassination and theft.

When Raul finished, he let the silence linger. He watched as Bonafaccio's face contorted in rage and concentration. Now it was Bonafaccio's turn to twist the kaleidoscope of reason. Ultimately, it was Romelli who couldn't contain himself.

"Jesus, Boss!" he blurted. "Can you believe that old bast—"

Bonafaccio held up his hand, mandating quiet, still weighing Raul's story. Another full minute passed as he kept his head down and massaged his temples. Finally, he looked up.

"Okay," he said, his voice weary and preoccupied, "back to the diamonds. Like I said, you've got a choice. Five mil or the boxes of cigars with the diamonds. Since I doubt you've got five mil stashed away, I suppose it'll have to be the diamonds, right?"

Raul searched Bonafaccio's eyes, the matador assessing the bull, as he sought the subtle blur of confusion that was key to the success of bolder moves. Satisfied the earlier flame had dimmed, he knew it was time to thrust the *estoque*—another moment of truth.

"What you and your butchers did here last night was murderous waste," Raul began in a low voice, his eyes fixed on his clenched hands. He looked up, his voice rising. "Yes, I have the Don Salazarios with the diamonds. Gessleman's foolish greed let them slip through his fingers, and he traded them to me for cigars in pretty wrappers. I discovered their treasure in a few I brought to Kingston and was returning to get the rest. Instead I found the carnage of your ignorance."

Raul stood, now towering over Bonafaccio. "Paulo did not have to die!" he cried.

"I would have happily delivered the Don Salazarios to you in exchange for his life. He had so much to live *for,* a homeland to return to.

"Maybe, by your Code, your family was compelled to murder my father. But not Paulo! He took nothing from you. He was simply trapped for a moment between you and what you sought. Even your father would not have commanded his death for that."

Bonafaccio looked at Romelli. Raul sensed his adversary's confusion as control of the moment deteriorated in Raul's favor.

Raul placed his hands on the desk and leaned down, his face inches from Bonafaccio's.

"So, Señor *Don* Bonafaccio"—Raul spit the appellation with undisguised contempt—"Paulo's death will not pass without value being exchanged. Some good will come of his sacrifice." He straightened.

"Yes, you may have your diamond cigars, but you *will* pay for them. A fraction of their value: one million, five hundred thousand dollars."

Raul paused to gauge Bonafaccio's reaction. There was none. Encouraged, he continued. "You have the connections to, what is your word? Ah, 'fence,' like a gate.

You can 'fence' the diamonds, something that would be difficult and risky for me. Your profit will be millions, true? Consider the million five simply as a memorial to Paulo, something your own 'Code' requires for innocent victims."

Raul watched to see if the *estoque* had struck true.

Then, the matador peaking to his toes at the end of the thrust, he added, "Of course, you no doubt intend to kill me as you did Paulo. Perfect insurance that the diamonds are lost to you forever. Ask yourself, why would I dare confront you like this unless I was protected. Better still, ask *him!*" Raul nodded toward Romelli.

Joseph swiveled away from the desk and stood, stretching his arms behind his head and again rolling his neck.

"Tell you what," he said, finally, "you've given me a lot to think about, and I don't think so well on an empty stomach. While I've been waiting for you to show up, Mr. Romelli has shoveled down a meal or two. Not me. Let's go have that dinner. I could also use a drink and a good smoke. That shouldn't be any trouble, right?"

"Follow me," said Raul, heading for the stairs. The bull was down.

# TWENTY-NINE

RAUL'S EARLIER VISIT to the kitchen had inspired spectacular results. Tournedos of aged Venezuelan beef, braised asparagus with papaya and mango chutney, roasted yams stuffed with macadamia nuts and honeyed currants—all worked their magic on Joseph Bonafaccio's appreciative palate.

Careful to choose his moment while his guests remained captives of the meal, Raul selected a box from the credenza humidor spanning one wall of the room. "Have you ever had one of these?"

He opened the gold-edged box of Saint Luis Rey Double Coronas and offered its contents to Joseph and Dominick. They helped themselves and lit up.

Settling behind the glow of the large cigar, Joseph sighed with pleasure. Moments later, his expression clouded. "A damn shame to have to continue our business discussion," he said, "but that's why we're here." He took a long draw and filled the space above with fresh smoke.

"One million, five hundred thousand. That's a hell of a 'memorial.' Mind telling me how you got there?"

Raul smiled, his first that night. "Of course," he said, choosing his words. Joseph's present mood was that of a well-sated lion. Soon enough, the bull would surface and charge again. Raul could never reveal his true intentions to this man whose warped sense of honor, his "Code," would call for Raul's life.

"When our dealings are concluded, I intend to sell this restaurant. The embargo has killed my business as I can no longer get the Cuban cigars my customers demand. There is another business I have come to know because of this restaurant and my father's before it—beef. I have had my eye on a cattle ranch in Argentina for some time. I can buy it for one million dollars. The other five hundred thousand is for 'expenses.' As I said, look upon it as a memorial to Paulo; he was to be my partner."

Bonafaccio regarded Raul thoughtfully for a moment, then spoke. "Tell you what. Leave Mr. Romelli and me alone for five minutes. Then come back and we'll talk."

Joseph stood and began to pace the humidor wall, smoking the double corona with enthusiasm.

"Dominick," he began, "I see opportunity here. Something the guy just said hit home. *He* can't bring in Cuban cigars, but *we* sure as hell can. This embargo will work just like prohibition. You tell people they can't have something, and they want it even more. And they'll pay through the nose to get it.

"We've got the contacts, the organization. With just a few modifications we could corner the cigar import business! Cuban and *non*-Cuban cigars. We set up a dummy-front import business and use it to smuggle in the Cuban cigars. We shield ourselves so that the feds could never trace the operation to the Family. If they bust it, we just set up another one and keep going. Hell, that's why we have lawyers."

His vision unfolding before him, Joseph picked up speed.

"You know what's going to happen? Just last week the *Wall Street Journal* talked about how Partagas, Macanudo, and some of the other big cigar houses are already expanding into the Dominican Republic and Honduras with Cuban tobacco seeds and Cuban rollers. Hell, in a couple of years they're going to be growing the same leaves and rolling the same cigars as the Cubans.

"Two things are going to come of all this: Smuggled Cuban cigars will bring premium prices. And, as the copycat premium cigars made outside Cuba hit the United States, the wider availability of good cigars will heighten the mystique of the real thing. We'll play each end off the other as we dominate both markets—the contraband Cuban cigars and the premium copycats."

Joseph stopped pacing and faced his amused mentor.

"Dom; think of it! A nationwide network of warehouses and outlets, maybe even a mail-order business—J. B. Cigars."

Romelli tilted back, his role as a respected sounding board for Joseph's sometimes crazy notions well defined.

"Joseph, some of this actually makes sense. Might just be the change you've been looking for. You're right about one thing. It can easily be set up to run on a low-risk basis.

Hell, that's why God gave us corporations. The Don loved 'em. But there's something I don't understand."

"What's that?" Joseph snapped, ready with an answer to any objection.

"Salazar," Romelli responded. "What the hell does he have to do with any of this? Hell, you can go into the cigar business any time you want. We're *supposed* to be dealing with Salazar and the diamonds."

Joseph took a short puff off his cigar and broke into a broad grin. "Ahh, Dominick, that's the *real* beauty of this whole thing." He resumed his pacing.

"This *place,*" he said, flinging his arms, "a cigar restaurant, like a club. A whole chain of 'em. Cuban music, Cuban food, stage shows, gorgeous women, and, at the heart of all of it, our cigars. The name's a natural: Noches Cubanas, Cuban Nights. Hell, we've still got a Nevada gaming license. We'll open a new casino, just like we had in Havana! They're legalizing gambling in Jersey. We'll open one there, too."

Joseph collapsed in his chair, flushed with excitement. "Well?"

Dominick shook his head, smiling. There was a light knock on the door. "Yeah, come on in," said Joseph, grinning across the table.

Raul entered and stood inside the door, wary of Joseph's buoyancy. Dominick frisked him and nodded toward the table. Raul took his seat and waited. It was the bull's move.

"Okay," said Bonafaccio, suddenly serious. "Here's what I'll do. One million. You get your ranch in Argentina, and I get my three boxes of diamond cigars. That and the fact that you walk away from this is plenty of 'memorial.' You can name your ranch after the stubborn old fart."

Raul willed that his stone face did not betray his racing heart. Afraid his voice would, he kept silent.

"There's something else," Bonafaccio said, his tone low and laden with purpose.

*Why am I not surprised?* Raul asked himself. He prepared for whatever was coming.

"I want this place, Noches Cubanas, lock, stock, and barrel. The name, the restaurant, everything. And I want you to stay on as a consultant for, say, two years, while I open others like it around the country. Then go grow your cows."

*Madre de Dios,* thought Raul. The dead bull begs for another sword!

"You are serious, Señor? You want this restaurant?"

Joseph straightened. "Salazar, when it comes to business, I don't make jokes. Yeah, I want the restaurant. His eyes shifted to the vintage posters of Manolete and Ordonez that decorated the room.

Raul's mind reeled. A *recibiendo!* The one time out of hundreds when the matador plants himself, holds firm, and lets the bull impale itself with the force of its own angry momentum. Raul again called upon the discipline of the gaming table, keeping his face stoic and voice flat.

"All right, Señor Bonafaccio, we have an agreement. One million dollars—you get the cigars and Noches Cubanas." He paused. "I must have the money immediately to close the deal on the ranch. It will also serve as my insurance policy." Then he added, "This is much as before when your father took the business from my father, no?"

"No," said Bonafaccio quietly. "Not at all like before. Your father cheated us and lost. I think you're much smarter than that. I'll give you the money now, but then you're moving to New York. We'll premiere the jewel of our chain in Manhattan."

Bonafacio stood. "I'll get the money together when the banks open in the morning; you get the cigars. I'll call you by ten A.M. with instructions where we'll meet and make the exchange."

Raul smiled and lowered his eyes. "No, Señor. I think not. Maybe I *am* smarter than my father, or perhaps wiser after what your family did to him." Raul drew on his cigar, then let the hovering smoke soften his words.

"There is only one place I will deliver the cigars to you. Here, at Noches Cubanas. You may have seen the amigos gathered in the bar. They will be here when you give me the money and I give you the cigars. Only you and Señor Romelli will come. No bodyguards or other associates. I have seen the work of *your* amigos; now you must learn the ways of mine."

Raul rolled the long cigar between his thumb and fingers. "You see, Señor, these are the men who were in Dallas. They are professionals, just as your men. I guarantee no harm will come to you, just as they will guarantee none will come to me."

Joseph flashed a questioning glance toward Romelli. "It's okay, Boss. In his place, we'd do the same."

Romelli turned to Raul, who detected the glint of a new respect in the bodyguard's eyes.

"I don't think Señor Salazar wants a war with us. He just wants the money. No one wins with a war. If Señor Salazar's men harmed you, they'd all join him pushing up swamp grass. He knows that, right?"

Raul shrugged. "As you have said, in my place, you would do the same."

"That's settled then," said Bonafaccio. Then he paused, frowning. "You have the cigars here?" he asked.

"*Sí,*" Raul replied. "They are here, waiting for you and the money."

"Let's have a look at 'em," said Bonafaccio. "Maybe peel apart a few random samples. I'm not buying a pig in a poke."

Raul had never heard the expression but did not doubt its meaning. The bull was back on its feet. It was time for the *descabello,* the cross-barred killing sword used to take down a dying animal once and for all.

"That is regrettable," Raul said. "But as you apparently judge others by your own standards, I can see it will be necessary. For this, we must go downstairs. We will take some company. You understand, I am sure."

Leaving the dining room, Raul motioned to Jorgé in the bar. The celebration evaporated into the thick smoke overhead. Four dark men fell in wordlessly behind Raul, Bonafaccio, and Romelli. The entourage descended to the basement.

Raul unlocked the door to the humidified room and switched on the light. Before them stood rows of nearly bare shelves housing Raul's shrunken inventory of Cuban cigars. On the pine table, scrubbed clean of the previous night's grisly residue, sat three boxes of Don Salazario

Presidentes. Two were sealed. The third was open, revealing a gap of four cigars. In their space lay a square of velvet cloth bearing four shimmering stones.

"As you see, Señor, one box has been opened. I took four cigars to Kingston. Otherwise, everything is as it was."

Jorgé and his amigos craned their necks to get a better look. Their hushed exclamations broke the silence.

"These weren't here last night," Romelli said.

Raul nodded. "Ah, they would not be here tonight if they had been, would they? I wish, for Paulo's sake, that I *had* kept them here."

Bonafaccio stepped forward and dug into the open box, selecting two cigars from the bottom layer. He held them up against the overhead light, inspecting the distinctive silk bands.

"Hmmph." His attempt at concealing his admiration failed. He pulled a penknife from his pocket and laid the cigars on the table, the open knife suspended above them. Like a surgeon planning the first incision, he paused and looked up at Raul, who shrugged his shoulders.

"All I ask is that you do not cut the bands," said Raul. "Perhaps *something* of my grandfather's art can be salvaged from this unnecessary destruction."

Bonafaccio slipped the bands from each cigar and passed them to Raul. "Here. On me," he said. With that he neatly sliced each cigar from end to end.

The divided halves fell apart, still bound by thin hinges of leaf along the bottom surface. Near the end of each eviscerated cigar nestled a glittering gem. Bonafaccio freed the stones with the blade tip and gently laid them next to the others on the velvet patch.

He looked up at Raul. "So far, so good," he said, and picked up one of the sealed boxes. Raul suddenly reached forward and grabbed Bonafaccio's arm.

"Stop! This is too much. You tortured and murdered my father. You tortured and murdered Paulo. Now, in front of me, you wish to destroy these last survivors of my family's craft. I cannot watch you do this. After the money is paid, they will be yours to ruin. Until then, they are mine, and I will not see them torn to shreds simply because you do not trust me. You should at least do as *I* was planning to do before I discovered Paulo's body and realized that you would come for them."

"Oh? And what was that, friend?" asked Bonafaccio.

"I . . . I was going to smoke them," whispered Raul. "Quickly, at first, to get the money for the ranch; then, as I grew older, I was going to gradually smoke the remaining diamonds free."

Joseph Bonafaccio blinked, surveyed his unsmiling audience, and laughed. Romelli joined in, and the two of them leaned against each other, their laughter feeding itself, bringing tears. Soon, even Jorgé and his amigos were struggling to contain themselves.

Raul slammed his fist on the table, bringing the short session of mirth to an abrupt end. The six loose stones cascaded together. "Enough!" he shouted, glaring at the traitorous amigos.

"Because of the barbarism committed in this room last night, I can no longer think of it as a place of cheer. It is a room of death." He turned and faced Bonafaccio. "Do as you will with the rest of the cigars. Cut them all or smoke them in Hell. Just be here tomorrow with my one million dollars."

To Jorgé he said, "I will not watch this. You four stay here and see that these butchers do not cheat me by stealing what they find."

Raul left the room and went upstairs. He had thrust the *descabello*. Only time would tell if this time the bull stayed down for good.

Several minutes later, as Raul sipped a tumbler of 151-proof rum at the bar and made an angry show of finishing his cigar, he heard the group mount the stairs. Joseph entered the bar and gave Raul a jovial smack on the back.

"Well, I saw enough," he said. "Those are some cigars. I cut open six more and every one had a diamond. Think I'll take your advice and smoke the rest of them out. I'm satisfied, for now."

Raul turned to face him. "For now?" he asked. "What does that mean?"

Bonafaccio's eyes narrowed. "It means, *Señor,* that you're going to have a guest until I get to a bank and return with the money. I don't want any funny business going on with those cigars. In case you didn't notice, Dominick's still downstairs. He's bunking there tonight. I told him to be my guest and smoke one or two more of 'em if he wanted. He'll add the eggs inside to the pile. Oh, by the way, here's some more bands for your collection. I'm gonna keep the rest of 'em though. I've got some ideas."

Raul accepted the bands, shaking his head. "As you

wish," he said. He turned to Jorgé. "I suppose this means one of us will have to keep him company. I will go first. Come down and relieve me in a few hours." He slid from his stool and started for the stairs.

# THIRTY

JOSEPH BONAFACCIO WHISTLED as he strode through
the lobby of the Miami Hilton. The murals of reclining
Egyptian royalty lifted his spirits even higher, their art
deco contours reminiscent of Manhattan.

The Don would have been proud. Forging opportunity
while favorably concluding an important piece of unfin-
ished Family business smacked of his father's style. It also
charged him with a virile rush. In the fifteen minutes since
he'd left Noches Cubanas, Joseph had built upon his vision. Now he saw the cables of an illegal web stretching
from Mexico to Canada and, ultimately, to Cuba. Joseph
would be at the hub, manipulating, controlling, and fun-
neling the pride of Cuba to eager American smokers. No
chorus dancer had taken him to the high he felt as he
stepped up to the reception desk.

"Oh, Mr. Bonafaccio! We expected you some time
ago. Your suite is ready, and you have messages." The
clerk handed Joseph an envelope.

In his suite, Joseph opened the envelope and his mood darkened. Cornelius Gessleman had called five times for either he or Romelli. Each message was marked "urgent."

Joseph picked up the phone, prepared to ask the hotel operator to connect him with the Kentucky number. Then he changed his mind.

"Operator?"

"Yes, Mr. Bonafaccio."

"I want you to block my phone to all incoming calls except from one person, Dominick Romelli. Got that?"

"Yes, sir. No calls unless from Mr. Dominick Romelli. Will that be all, sir?"

"Yes. Good night."

There was no way, Joseph thought as he undressed, that he was going to risk talking on the telephone to the sonofabitch responsible for Kennedy's assassination. The Family needed to steer wide of that nut. He would leave the discussion to Dominick. Hell, Romelli could walk from a coal mine onto white sheets without leaving tracks.

Joseph turned on the TV and settled back on the bed, not really watching. The absorbing excitement of his cigar plans had blinded him to the other implications of the day's events. They involved Salazar and Gessleman.

Dominick had been right, as usual. Salazar should live, and not simply because the Don had thought so eight years earlier. Raul Salazar had demonstrated incredible nerve and operational talent in carrying out his dual mission for Gessleman. What was more, the way Raul had squared off with Joseph and Romelli had earned Joseph's respect. A negotiator and operator of that caliber was an asset to be cultivated, not eliminated.

That part of the Code mandating revenge for spilled blood did not call for the lives of skilled soldiers who simply carried out orders, or professionals who honored their contracts. After all, the loyalty of Bonafaccio soldiers to their generals had given the Family its muscle.

With the flickering TV images dancing before him, Joseph concluded that Raul Salazar and his amigos were immune for their part in the Kennedy business. But the immunity stopped there. When generals gave orders that violated the Code, it was *their* heads that should roll. *Yes,* he thought, *Cornelius Gessleman and his son-in-law will soon hear from Dominick Romelli.*

Well satisfied with the day's work, and flushed with his new-found resolve as the Family's helmsman, Joseph Bonafaccio Jr. finally let Johnny Carson's wisecracks lead him toward sleep. He had found his destiny.

"The young Don is serious about buying this place?" Raul asked, taking a quick mental inventory of the depleted cigar stock housed alongside the wine cellar. In one month, maybe a month and a half at most, they would all be gone. Without a steady supply from Cuba, there was no hope for Noches Cubanas.

"Like the man said, he does not joke about business," replied Romelli. He sat forward for a moment, studying Raul. Finally, his professional curiosity got the better of him. "Tell me, how did you pull it off, that action in Dallas? And why, for crissakes, did your man use that goddamn Mannlicher? That was a tough enough shot for a marksman with a scoped .308. But *that* sloppy relic? Jesus."

Unexpectedly, another bull had suddenly charged the ring.

Raul was exhausted and doubted his ability to continue the *torero*'s dance much longer. Besides, *this* bull possessed a deadly advantage, a knowledge of weapons. Raul did not know a Mannlicher from a BB gun. He sighed and caressed the nearest box of Don Salazarios. It was time for the *remate*, that master pass of conclusion where the matador executes a subtle, but confusing, twirl of the cape. The bull, perplexed and still, is left defenseless to its fate.

"Señor Romelli," he began slowly, "it is enough for now that you know we succeeded. We chose our tools for good reasons. History confirms the wisdom of our choice. Someday, if you and I come to know one another better, I may share these things with you. Until then . . ."

Raul opened the lid of the box. He raised two of the cigars and said, "Will you join me in liberating two more of Señor Bonafaccio's jewels?"

# THIRTY-ONE

"REALLY, MR. BONAFACCIO, I would feel much better about this if you would let us arrange an escort." The frowning bank manager seemed unable to release Joseph's hand after their farewell shake. After all, one million dollars of his bank's money was about to disappear through the door, strapped to the waist of a stranger. Though Joseph's impeccable credentials had immediately checked out, this was not an everyday transaction.

"Please, at our expense," he added, clasping his other hand over the handshake, forming a vice.

"I appreciate your concern," said Joseph, wriggling free. "I have my own security people. We—ah—are used to dealing with these situations."

The banker's blatant curiosity concerning the wire transfer had irritated Joseph. Bankers all suffered from the same dilemma: Their desire to know details was always at war with their need to be insulated from them. There had been no questions asked and no answers offered.

"Thanks for your help; I'll be in touch soon. I'm buying a business in this area and have plans for expansion. We'll be needing your services."

Joseph turned away and headed briskly for the main door.

Stepping from the air-conditioned comfort of the bank into the muggy morning, he gave the money belt a reassuring pat and crossed to the parked rental car. He felt naked without Romelli and conjured a thousand pairs of eyes boring through his linen coat. Impatient with himself, he shook off the temptation to accept the banker's offer and unlocked the door.

Sending the two soldiers home had been mandatory. Once a soldier did a job, he cleared town, no exceptions. The messy work on the old man two nights earlier had triggered the policy, though Joseph now wished he had kept them around. Driving around Miami with a million-dollar waistband did not seem particularly bright.

He pulled into traffic quickly, anxious to get the day's business done. Carrying three boxes of cigars home to Manhattan seemed a lot safer than wearing one million dollars.

Raul awakened to sounds at the top of the stairs. He immediately longed for a shower and a shave. When Jorgé had come down to relieve his vigil over the cigars with Romelli, the night's adrenaline had compelled him to stay. Now, at 10:30 A.M., the stale odor of three cloistered men smoking cigars in a small room for eight hours had sapped that energy.

He swung his legs off the cot and could not help but

smile. Jorgé and Romelli were sitting across the table from each other, a dozen or so cigar stubs crowding the ashtray. In the middle, on the swatch of black velvet, the few gems that had been there when he'd closed his eyes three hours earlier had ripened into a shimmering cluster. Jorgé and Romelli, each mouthing a glowing stub, sat watching each other like cats in opposite yards as the noise at the top of the stairs became descending footsteps.

"Hey!" boomed Joseph Bonafaccio, "you guys have been busy! Look at all those little beauties!" Then he stopped, wrinkled his nose, and laughed. "Jesus Christ! Smells worse than a forgotten gym locker down here. What pigs."

Joseph ran an index finger through the stones, gently turning them, letting the light from overhead play off their edges.

Romelli stood and stretched. Joseph took his chair and pulled an envelope from his coat pocket. He unfolded a hand-printed sheet of paper on the table next to the stones.

"I drew up an agreement this morning—for the sale of the restaurant," he said, looking at Raul. "Nothing complicated. The lawyers can do that later. Just something for each of us to sign to give them something to work with." He pushed the paper toward Raul, who stood up from the cot, blinking the sleep from his brain. He was back in the bullring.

Bonafaccio unbuttoned his coat and reached for his waist. Raul saw Jorgé tense, then relax as Joseph's hand surfaced. Bonafaccio's fingers gripped the tongue of a padded belt, which he uncoiled from around his waist. He dumped it on the table with a flourish and unsnapped three of its long pockets, revealing thick layers of bills. Then he took a cigar from the open box.

"You know, Salazar," Joseph said, "maybe your plan wasn't so crazy after all. Why *not* smoke out those diamonds? Give us something to do back in Manhattan, hey, Dom?" Romelli nodded, not with enthusiasm.

"Well, go ahead! Count it!" Joseph laughed. "It's not some snake. It's only money." He cut the cigar and lit it.

*Who,* thought Raul, was *this man who could laugh at giving up one million dollars, who smelled so fresh and wore the clothes of a movie star? Could this be the deadly bull he had waltzed with hours earlier?*

Then he remembered that Joseph had presided over Paulo's torture and murder in the same room not forty-eight hours before. Had he been dressed in pressed linen and smelling of Bay Rum even then, as he'd taken in Paulo's sweating agonies?

Raul stepped to the table and gestured with his head to Jorgé, who stood. Raul took his chair and unsnapped the remaining pockets of the belt. He pulled out several thick packets of bills, riffled them like decks of cards, drew in the acrid smell of new money, and went to work.

Ten minutes later, his mind numbed by the monotony of counting, Joseph's happy shout snapped him back to the moment.

"Hey! There it is!" Bonafaccio brushed the glowing tip of his cigar against the ashtray and laughed as a buried gem tumbled from the embered point. "Christ!" he exclaimed, "Can you imagine the effect this would have on a dame? Now, *that's* something to think about."

Finally, surrounded by piles of counted bills, Raul finished. *Thank God,* he thought, *seeing that Bonafaccio was struggling with whether to waste another of his diamond cigars in Raul's cellar or save it for the fleshy pleasures of Manhattan.*

"You have a pen, Señor?" he asked Joseph, reaching for the document on the table. Bonafaccio pulled a pen from his jacket pocket and handed it to him. Raul signed the paper and let it flutter back to the table. For the first time, he was a stranger in Noches Cubanas, now owned by Hudson Valley Properties, whatever that was.

"So, we are done. It is over," Raul said solemnly. Then he added, "At great cost."

Bonafaccio stood and spoke as he bundled the stones together in their cloth. He nodded to Romelli, who gathered together the three boxes of Don Salazarios.

"Well, Señor Salazar, look at it this way. You had two jobs to do: to get the president and his cigars. You used one job to do the other, a means to an end. Like you say, at great cost. Not one I would have agreed with, but sure as hell effective.

"Like you, I had a job to do, to reclaim my family's assets. The old man who died here was a means to that end, another great cost. We are even. It was business, that's all, just business."

Raul choked back the rage in his throat, rage at himself. This dandied gangster was offering as justification for Paulo's murder the very ruse Raul had used to dupe Gessleman and the congressman!

Bonafaccio continued. "I've got to tell you that your

entire operation, the work in Dallas and getting the cigars, was a masterpiece. You've got the whole goddamned country buzzing around, investigations, commissions, who knows what else? It would be a shame to see that talent wasted on cows. Go buy your ranch. Hell, everyone needs a hobby. But your life, your *real* life, is with *me*. Action, you love it. Anyone can see that. After you come to New York, you'll agree."

The arena filled with a roar as Raul stood, motionless. The bull was down, quivering spasms of death rolling in waves along its bloodied back. The *presidente* of the fight stood in his box, responding to the fluttering *pañuelos*, a sea of waving white handkerchiefs. Trumpets blared in acknowledgment of his triumph. The *presidente* dropped his own handkerchief, signaling the award for a great kill, *dos orejas*, two ears. Raul took the first steps of his *vuelta al ruedo*, his victorious circuit of the arena.

He shrugged. "Perhaps. We shall see."

"Good!" exclaimed Bonafaccio. "Very good. Dom, let's go home. Salazar, a lawyer will call you in a day or so to finish the restaurant deal. You wrap things up here; then you come to New York. We'll have a place for you."

Bonafaccio stopped and turned at the door. "And Salazar?"

"Yes?" answered Raul.

"Don't even think of *not* coming to New York. It's part of our deal, remember? You must know by now that no one, *no one*, reneges on a deal with us. Understand?"

Raul nodded, still circling the ring, his cap raised to the adoring crowd.

Jorgé and Raul watched from Raul's office as the black sedan pulled away.

"Quickly, Jorgé, tell the amigos and staff to meet with us in the dining room in half an hour. Then come upstairs and help me. We have much to do and time is short. Those two will return here within days. They will not be so friendly, and they will not be alone."

Thirty minutes later Raul and Jorgé came down the stairs. Raul carried a box. The good-natured buzz of camaraderie hushed as Raul folded his arms and stood before his friends and employees.

"Amigos," he began, "many years ago in Cuba, my father took certain actions he thought necessary to protect himself from the gangsters who stole his business. Well, those men he so offended have long memories. They have visited me and, as before, are taking over *this* business."

Raul studied the faces of his staff.

"You may think that they will need cooks, waiters, busboys, and helpers. But I am afraid that will not be so." He paused.

"You see, when they return here, it will not be to claim their new business. It will be to kill me and everyone associated with this place."

Amid gasps and shocked faces, he continued.

"You brave sailors who faced the ocean's terror to avoid Castro's jails must now face another challenge, but it will be a more pleasant one, I promise you."

He read the trust in their eyes and felt a warm rush from what he was about to do.

"You must all leave here today and never return. You should move from Miami and forget Noches Cubanas. I have destroyed all records with your names and addresses, and the Mafia gangsters will never find you if you do as I say."

Now, facing looks that questioned and puzzled over what had been asked of them, Raul lifted the box he had brought down from his office and placed it on the table in front of him. He opened it to reveal a stack of sealed, white envelopes. Jorgé began handing them out.

"In these envelopes," Raul continued, "you will find the cash you need to move and start a new life, hopefully a better one." Raul circulated, shaking hands and hugging his staff. Then he turned to Jorgé and his amigos.

"You three and Pedro have been well paid for your recent services. But knowing how you go through money, and because what I have done has put you at greater risk, I have prepared a bonus for you." He withdrew four more envelopes from his jacket pocket.

"Bonafaccio has seen your faces, and you know what he believes you have done. When he returns to Miami, he will be seeking revenge. He must find none of you. There is enough money here for you to disappear, and I urge you to do that. Jorgé, you must explain this to Pedro and see that he gets his money."

Jorgé nodded, passing envelopes to the other two men.

"And what of you, Raul?" Jorgé asked. "What will you do?"

Raul smiled. "I think I will go fishing, no?"

# THIRTY-TWO

Dep. Luther Ruggles prickled in sweaty discomfort. He had stalled as long as he dared. His brother-in-law, Ernie, was pressing for an answer, and his wife, Patti-Ann, had told him that morning not to bother coming home until it was done.

"Uh, Hiram, got a minute?" he asked, standing at the doorway to the constable's office.

Hiram Thorpe looked up from his report. "Yes, Luther?"

Luther shifted from one foot to the other, not sure whether he should come in and sit down. He decided he'd stay near the door, on his feet, able to flee as soon as he broke the terrible news.

Hiram peered over his bifocals. "Somethin' botherin' you, Luther?" he asked.

*Shucks,* thought Luther, *I'm in it now. Have to see it through.*

"Well, Hiram, it's like this. You remember Patti-Ann's brother, Ernie?"

Hiram nodded. It was hard to forget Ernie. Any grown man who played with toy soldiers should be put away, he had told Luther.

"Well, Ernie's got this plan. Me and Patti-Ann think it's a pretty good one."

Hiram rubbed his eyes, preparing himself.

"Thing is," Luther continued, "it involves me and Patti-Ann pullin' out and movin' to Portland, Maine. See, Ernie wants to open this model shop and wants me to come in as . . ."

Hiram sat upright. Luther knew he had his full attention now. Oh, this was going to be worse than he had feared.

"Luther, you tellin' me you're quittin'?"

"Well, Hiram, Patti-Ann wants to be closer to her folks, and it's a pretty good opportunity for me. But I won't do it if it leaves you hangin'. You know that. I can hold off for a time 'til we find a good replacement. I'll stay and help you train him even."

Hiram stood and came around the desk. Luther took a step backward but then was caught up in Hiram's thick arm as it wrapped around his shoulders like a hairy anaconda.

"Hell, boy, when opportunity knocks, you got to answer! Don't you worry 'bout me. You do what's best for you and Patti-Ann. I'll fix it with the county so's you're paid for one month, and you can just leave right now."

Hiram's hand slid down and he unpinned Luther's

badge. "There. It's done. Luther Ruggles, civilian. Good luck, son." Hiram took Luther's hand and pumped a vigorous shake.

"Now, just sign this Civil Service form and it's official." Hiram whisked a sheet from his top desk drawer.

Luther scrawled his signature, stunned Hiram was taking the blow so well. Still, he wanted to get out of there before it really sank in. Sometimes Hiram had an awful temper.

Hiram watched Luther almost skip down the sidewalk. He returned to his desk, chuckled, and picked up the phone.

"Oscar? Hiram Thorpe. No more break-ins? Good. Didn't think there would be. Say, Oscar, is that Pedro Vasquez still hangin' around? You know, the Latin fella that did some work out there and was sweet on Felicia? He is? Good. Tell him to stop by and see me, would you? The sooner the better."

After hanging up, Hiram reopened his desk drawer and began rummaging. "Ah, here they are," he said, satisfied. "APPLICATION FOR EMPLOYMENT," he read aloud. "Liked that boy from the moment I met him. Should make a fine deputy. Good instincts and fast on his feet. Be a good husband for Felicia, too."

Hiram settled back and lit a Muniemaker. The stack of cigar boxes from the Gessleman place filled the corner of his office. He would make *that* phone call soon enough, he thought. The newspapers would tell him when.

# THIRTY-THREE

"PHEW. PAULO, MI amigo, you are not smelling so good. Time to get you out of here before someone gets curious."

Raul surveyed his preparations. Food, water, nautical chart, fuel, oh yes, plenty of fuel. For this trip he had filled both tanks.

Satisfied all was ready, Raul cast off both lines, climbed to the flying bridge and slipped the boat in gear. *Ahh,* he thought, *a great day to start a new life.*

The *Don Salazario* idled out of the marina and nosed toward open water. Reaching the harbor mouth, Raul brought her up to full throttle. The sleek cruiser rose to a plane and danced across the blue water, her bow pointed due south.

The telephone in Joseph Bonafaccio's bedroom was off-limits to all but Dominick Romelli. *This had better be pretty damned important, Dom,* Joseph thought, sliding his hand along the creamy thigh nestled against him. He reached to answer the muffled ring that had interrupted his pleasure.

True to Joseph's forecast, the diamond cigars proved irresistible to the Rockettes he had selected to share a smoke. Word spread quickly among the leggy dancers of the glittering good fortune that could brighten the life of a girl willing to share the communion of Joseph Bonafaccio's bed and a cigar. Having nurtured the image, Joseph had begun conserving the diamond cigars, substituting ordinary ones on a random basis for his pretty guests. "Diamond Roulette," he had dubbed the game, and, sure enough, the uncertain outcome often excited a heightened performance from his date.

"What is it, Dominick?" asked Joseph, not hiding his irritation.

"Something that can't wait, Joseph. Sorry." The gloom in Romelli's voice told him nothing. Sounding sombrous was Dom's job.

Joseph hoped it wasn't a snag with the movie studio they were trying to unload. The deal had been shaky before the trip to Miami. Since their return, he had shored up the weak spots and the sale appeared certain. Once it closed, he would focus on his new venture.

"I've got Herman Meyer on the phone, Joseph. I think you'd better get in here."

Joseph slid from between the satin sheets and wrapped himself in his robe.

"Back in a minute, doll. Got to talk to a man about some sparklers," he said. Meyer was probably balking at price. Predictable. He stepped into his slippers and padded out of the bedroom and into the office suite.

"Good evening, Herman. Hell of a time to be bickering about diamonds, isn't it? I thought we agreed on a price over a week ago—thirty thousand per."

"Yes, Joseph, we did agree on a price. For diamonds. *These*, what Dominick brought me yesterday, are *not* diamonds. They are some of the best cut glass I have ever seen, but diamonds they are not. The work is exquisite, like that of Javier Menendez himself."

The elevator cable snapped at the one hundredth floor, and Joseph Bonafaccio plummeted through space. Air escaped his chest with the whoosh of a compressed bellows.

"Joseph?" Meyer's voice queried from another planet.

Fragments showered the room as Joseph smashed the receiver against the wall.

"GODDAMNIT, FINGERS! GET AN ARMY! WE'RE GOING TO ATOMIZE THAT MISERABLE SONOFA-BITCH AND HIS WHOLE FUCKING MOB!"

# THIRTY-FOUR

CORNELIUS GESSLEMAN GENTLED the mare with a soothing purr, the silky tone masking the menace in his heart.

"Soon, precious, soon. Mr. Bonafaccio, Mr. Romelli, and their friends just paid me a visit on their way to Miami. We had a cigar and a *very* productive chat. They agreed my requests were reasonable and assured me they would be carried out. The money I paid them was a *bargain*. You'll win it all back for me next spring, won't you? Yes, yes, I have your treat."

The horse nuzzled his hand, seeking the carrot in its bony clutch.

Around them, dormant trunks rose from mounded pastures, blanketed with a luminous dusting of new snow. Leafless, dark branches fused with the low sky, forming an uncertain, fitful canopy.

The horse persisted, its lips probing the clenched fist.

"Patience, my love, patience. Soon, I promise. Think

of it! Both of them, Salazar and Wesley. And they said they would make that thief Salazar sing a tune first, before he coughs up my money *and* those three boxes of relic cigars."

Cornelius climbed onto the lower rung of the fence, and tantalized the horse further by snuggling the carrot behind his back. The animal strained its lowered muzzle around its owner in search of the concealed prize.

"Convenient, isn't it? Wesley at home in Miami. Both of them together."

As Gessleman hitched higher on the fence, he steadied himself with the horse's neck, still teasing with the carrot. In the distance, where white fields met the gray sky, a blur of fresh snow flurries stirred and advanced toward them.

"Then another funeral, I suppose," he said, mocking a somber tone. "Wonder if I can't talk Margaret into just a small memorial service?"

He looked past the horse's head to the approaching mist of snow and vexed the horse one more time with the carrot before yielding.

When the mare's white neck erupted in a bloody font, Cornelius Gessleman was already dying, the same .308 slug having passed through his own neck a millisecond earlier.

"Yeah, Dom, it was a great shot. But shooting the horse? Jesus."

The Cadillac cruised sedately through Madison County, having left the exsanguinated corpses of Cornelius Gessleman and his Derby hopeful half an hour behind.

Romelli wasn't amused. "Joseph, in this business, you

take the shot when it's there. I could have been hours poking around the guy's farm waiting for a chance like that. We don't have that kind of time.

"Salazar's not going to wait for you to send him a letter telling him how pissed off you are. You said you wanted to get Gessleman off the books, that it would make you feel better since he'd started this whole thing. Well? Feel better? You got him *and* his three hundred grand. Worth the detour?"

Joseph settled into the thick seat. "Yeah, I guess. Too bad we can't tell anyone about it—that we just took out the guy who's responsible for assassinating the president."

Then, inspired, he turned and said, "Dom, you're a national *hero,* and no one's giving you a medal! Jesus. Here, take the money. Your country owes you."

Romelli stuffed the envelope in his jacket pocket and opened the door of the bar cabinet in the rear of the front seat. He poured two shots of amber liquid into crystal glasses and handed one to Joseph.

"Well, here's to me, then. A great American hero. Might as well toast me with good Kentucky bourbon, considering where we are."

He leaned forward and tapped the driver's shoulder. "Hey, Angelo, what say we get off this back road and onto a highway while we're still young enough to piss, hey? I'd like to make Miami before next summer."

*Yeah,* he thought, *let's get there.* Through the scope, he had seen Gessleman's body crumple, the crack of the rifle still rising in the crisp, winter air. Until that moment, he had not realized just how much he, too, missed the old ways.

Romelli turned and looked through the rear window. The two other Cadillacs were close behind, a convoy of eight killers intent on blasting Noches Cubanas into an echo of the Alamo.

# THIRTY-FIVE

"EMPTY! WHAT DO you mean *empty?*" Joseph Bonafaccio's head and shoulders filled the lowered window as Dominick Romelli bent to explain.

"Joseph, the place is cleaned out. No employees, no food, booze, or cigars. The cupboards are bare. There was an envelope addressed to you taped to the office door. Here."

Joseph tore it open and unfolded the letter inside. The handwritten printing was neat and concise.

*Joseph Bonafaccio Jr:*

*You murdered my father, stole his business and that of my grandfather, leaving him to die a broken man. Then you murdered my great friend, Paulo. You call all of this "business."*

*Though you think you know your "business," you know nothing of life. And I think you do not know so much about your business after all.*

*I fought you like a bull, but as it turned out you were just a stupid cow. Like a cow, you can now chew on your reward. I kept another Don Salazario from you, a very special one. It is in my office.*

*Adios,*
*Raul Salazar*

Joseph folded the letter, pinching each crease twice. If, *when,* they snagged Raul Salazar, he would relish making him eat it. He stepped from the car. "Let's take a look in Señor Salazar's office."

Fifteen minutes later, standing in the rubble of their search, Dominick spotted the picture. There on the wall, the perky lift of *Don Salazario's* bow topped a foaming crest as Raul grinned from the flying bridge and waved a skipper's cap.

They stared at the picture for a full minute. Joseph spoke first.

"Dom, the bastard thinks that by running off to Cuba or somewhere in the Caribbean, he can escape us. Not so, my friend, not so. We may be out of Cuba, but we still have connections. It doesn't matter *who's* in charge—a bribe's a bribe. We'll scour the place until we find him. When we do . . ."

Romelli nodded as Joseph finished.

". . . well, Señor Salazar is going to learn that we know our business *very* well. I swear it'll be the *last* thing he learns. He's younger and healthier than the old man. He'll last longer to enjoy the lesson. Let's go. I've seen enough."

As they passed through the bar, one of Bonafaccio's men picked up a bottle of liquor and hurled it into the back bar, shattering glasses and bottles.

"Hey! Goddamnit, cut that out! I own this place!" Bonafaccio shouted, glaring at the dark-suited killer.

They stepped into a bright Miami afternoon, and Joseph blinked, adjusting to the change. On the corner, a few feet away, a barefoot boy was hawking newspapers. The front page arrested his attention.

"Jesus!" exclaimed Joseph, hooking the boy's arm. "Dominick, look at this. It's him!"

There was only one thing on the Spanish language paper they understood: a headline-captioned photo of Raul Salazar.

"Kid," said Romelli, "you speak English?"

"*Sí* Señor, I do, very well," the boy replied, twisting away from Joseph. "You want to buy a paper?"

"Sure," said Romelli, handing the boy a five-dollar bill. "Do me a favor," he said, pointing to the photograph. "Read to me in English what it says about this man."

The boy hesitated, eyeing Joseph.

"I'm sorry kid," Joseph said. "I just got excited when I saw my friend's picture on your paper."

The boy's eyes widened. "You know Señor Salazar?" he asked, his voice pinched with excitement.

"Yes, we know him. We are—old amigos," Joseph answered. "We came to visit, but he's moved away. Now, tell us; what's the paper say about him?"

"Señor, I do not have to read it to you. Everyone knows what it says. Señor Salazar blew up. Boom! He was out on his boat and it exploded. He did not move away. He is dead."

Joseph snatched the newspaper, scanning, searching. No kid with dirty feet could rob him of his vengeance.

Romelli laid a hand on Joseph's shoulder. "Joseph, the police. We need answers. Let's go."

Two hours later, in a small park across from the Key Biscayne Police Station, Dominick Romelli slid into the front seat of the Cadillac and turned to face his employer.

"Happened three days ago, the day after we flew out of here. He bought some bait at the marina. The harbormaster saw his boat leave. Looked like he was alone. He was rigged for fishing.

"About an hour later, there was an explosion eight miles off shore. By the time the Coast Guard got there, the boat had burned to the water line and the hull was sinking. There were pieces of his body, burned beyond recognition. And, oh yeah, one other thing."

"What's that?" asked Joseph, crushing Raul Salazar's letter.

"There was money floating around the wreck. Lots of it. They recovered over twenty-five thousand dollars, still in the bands from the bank in Miami. They think it must have had something to do with drugs. They don't have a clue what really happened."

Joseph opened the door, stepped from the car, and stretched. He started down the sidewalk. Romelli exited and fell in alongside.

"So, Boss, that's that, I suppose."

Joseph shook his head. "Not quite, Dom," he said.

Romelli looked puzzled. Joseph stopped and turned. "There's *still* the goddamn congressman, Dominick," Joseph said patiently. "We got paid to take out the assassinating-cigar-stealing sonofabitch, and by God, we're gonna do it. We owe it to our country."

Joseph turned and marched with renewed vigor back to the Cadillac.

# THIRTY-SIX

IT HAD BEEN hard finding a *Washington Post* on the Cape. Finally, Hiram Thorpe had subscribed, sure that the item he had been waiting for would appear there. He was right.

"Peter Swindt."

"Oh, Mr. Swindt. You're still there, are you? Good. Thought you'd be working late tonight. We need to talk."

Hiram Thorpe tilted back in his chair, the creaking mechanism defying several laws of physics as it balanced his girth at a delirious angle.

"Who is this?" Swindt asked curtly.

"This is Hiram Thorpe. *Constable* Hiram Thorpe, up here in Cape Cod. Barnstable County. Remember me now?"

A sigh. Then, "Yes, Constable. I'm, uh, rather busy right now. What's up?"

Hiram let out a long blow of smoke as he took the Swisher Sweet from his mouth and laid it on the ashtray in front of him. He tilted forward.

"Yep, I'll bet you're busy all right. Clearin' out, correct? The New Broom and all that. Been doin' some of that myself." Hiram looked proudly at Pedro's desk, now cleared of Luther's airplane magazines and model parts. "Took awhile, though. Damned Civil Service, know what I mean?"

"Look, Sheriff . . ."

"Constable," Hiram corrected.

*"Constable . . ."*

Hiram warmed, enjoying his success.

". . . whatever it is you want to say, get on with it. I have to catch a plane to New York."

"No kidding. Just like that, huh? Fly from D.C. to New York. Can't be more than a couple hours' drive, is it? How long's it take to fly?"

"I really do *not* have time for this. Now tell me what you want, or I'm hanging up."

Hiram figured he'd stretched the string taut enough. Time to wrap the package.

"Well, remember those cigars that were never stolen during that break-in that never happened? Thought you'd like to know I'm lookin' at all forty boxes of 'em, not ten feet from me. Just wondered what you wanted me to do with 'em, you bein' the family's official spokesman and all."

Another sigh. "Is that all? I thought I made myself very clear about that. As far as I and the family are concerned, any cigars you have, you can burn. Got that? *Burn* them. Get rid of them. End of chapter. End of conversation. Good-bye."

The outer door burst open and Dep. Pedro Vasquez entered, brushing fresh snow from his shiny deputy's jacket and stamping slush from his new fur-topped boots.

"Pedro! Just in time! We got us an official duty to perform. Have to destroy some confiscated contraband."

Hiram stood and walked over to the stacked boxes. His forefinger danced down the columns of bright labels. Stopping at a box of Ramon Allones Coronas, he removed it, slit the seal with a letter opener, and pried it open.

"Might as well start here," he said. "Probably only take us ten years or so."

At first, shards of the erupted boat drifted apart, still obeying cosmic laws of explosion. Then, as maxims of the sea prevailed, they congregated in a loose village of fragments, borne by currents, and drifted as a mass in compliance with the ocean's will.

Foodstuffs, buoyed by their packaging, floated on the surface. Scavengers from above and below gorged themselves on Raul's meals as sharks and emboldened bonita threaded through the flotsam. Gulls and terns marked the course of the wreckage from the air.

Abandoned by the Coast Guard and the police, its devastation having yielded all the clues they could gather, the orphaned remnants of the *Don Salazario* continued to drift, its master now the sea.

The first of the gaunt, browned men on makeshift rafts spotted the feeding birds from two miles away. The swells of southerly current lifted them toward the birds as it carried them from Cuba, to Florida and sanctuary in the United States.

"Amigos!" the leader shouted to his comrades. "Food!"

He leaned from the ragtag collection of oil drums and wooden crates that had been his home for eight days and in amazement, swept up an orange and a small box of cereal wrapped in cellophane. Then he spotted something else, bobbing just below the surface. His brown arm dipped into the water a second time, and he brought up a bundle of bills. He suppressed a second call to his companions. *They will each,* he thought, *in turn, encounter this strange welcome from their new homeland.*

Eighty miles south of the *Don Salazario*'s splintered remains, a new group of rafters awakened to the perils of their voyage. Eleven skinny young men, seasick and frightened, watched the great sharks cruise closer as a new storm formed in the northeast and began to bear down on them. Panicked, they struggled to cluster together, their sad eyes filled with parting for those who would not see the next sunrise.

The leader straightened, his attention drawn to a speck on the darkening horizon. It grew, its shape changing and eluding him as the distance closed. Then, as the shape danced across the whitecaps, he heard the bee's buzz of a small outboard motor. An inflatable boat! Coming straight toward them! Was it Castro's police?

"Amigos!" he called. "Over there!"

Eleven pairs of eyes now strained to make out the craft bearing down on them.

"It is too small to be the police!" called one of them. "There is only one man."

Seizing respite from the dark seas rolling under them, the young voyagers stared toward the intruder. Then the leader started to laugh. "He is smoking a cigar! A very grand cigar!"

The rest joined in his laughter, their plight on the swelling ocean now minimized. This madman careening toward them in a rubber boat smoking a huge cigar had made the moment a circus.

"Amigos!" called Raul, slowing and maneuvering the inflatable dinghy through the sorry flotilla. "You must postpone your journey! There is a storm coming. You will only feed the sharks!"

"We cannot go back!" called the leader. "Castro freed us from jail to leave. We will rot in prison or be shot if we go back. Without jobs, we are garbage to him."

Raul continued to circle among the tubes, his eyes scanning each occupant. Then he cut the motor to an idle.

"Here!" he shouted, passing a line over the side of the inflatable, as it trailed through the group.

"There are jobs for you at my new restaurant or at the clinic my Rosa will build. Castro and Cuba need us now more than ever. Those who wish to return, grab the rope and come with me."

With each hand that grasped the line, Raul felt Rosa and Cuba reaching across the water, drawing him home. Finally, the added burden of his motley convey in tow, he twisted the outboard's throttle and slowly took up the slack. Unable to make his previous speed, he surveyed the approaching storm and gauged his now impeded progress.

Satisfied they would make landfall ahead of the

weather, Raul opened the waterproof container that filled the center of his craft. Resting on top of the bundles of bills was a large cedar box embossed with the name, EL ROSARIO-FABRICA DE TABACO. He lit a fresh Don Salazario and passed it to the leader.

"We will touch the beach well ahead of the storm!" he said, as the skinny, dark man accepted the great cigar. "Smoke this carefully and give me what you find inside. It will be your gift to Rosa and her children." Laughing at the man's confusion, Raul patted his buttoned shirt pocket, cradling three diamonds already freed on his voyage south.

"El Balsero!" Raul shouted, suddenly inspired. A perfect name for his new restaurant. *But, who knows,* he thought, *maybe Castro will have something to say about that.* "La Rosa," he said to himself, savoring the way her name slipped from his tongue. Now *there's* a name. He gave the squall to the north a last look and turned to face the land and the woman he loved.